Miranda

To all readers who enjoy my writing

Chapter One

Miranda walked briskly along the street, trying to appear cheerful and energetic. Could this be the first day of her new life? Just over a month ago, she had learned that there were to be redundancies at work and that she was among the first five to go. She had worked her notice, cleared her desk, and left. At thirty, she knew that she should rise to the challenge and find other employment as quickly as she could, but she felt dejected and without direction. She had already applied for a number of jobs, but with an absence of enthusiasm.

'Something has to change,' she told the magpie that flew over her head. She watched it land on a nearby roof, joining a row of others that had already assembled there.

She saw one of her neighbours approaching.

'Nice day,' he observed as he passed her.

Miranda managed to stretch her face into a failed smile. 'It isn't a nice day,' she muttered under her breath. 'Why do people insist on saying such stupid things? It's December. It's cold and damp. I haven't got a job, and I don't know where I'm going...'

Miranda lived in a compact red-brick terraced house on the street that ran through the village of Brentley. She had bought it four years ago, and had gradually made it feel like home. The front door opened directly from the street, straight into a living room, with a kitchen at one end that had a door leading into a back yard. An open staircase led up to the bathroom and bedroom. Her neighbours were pleasant, but she had never managed to develop anything more than a superficial relationship with any of them. This had not really bothered her before, but today she found that it annoyed her intensely.

She had a sudden impulse to turn round and run up to him

shouting 'What do you mean by "nice day"? It's horrible!' But she forced herself to continue in the direction of the post office, where she planned to buy stamps for her Christmas cards.

Despite an overuse of tinsel, the post office appeared drab. There was a long queue for the counter, and as Miranda waited she scanned the covers of the magazines in the rack alongside her. The promises of amazing diets and the photographs of celebrity weddings offered no inspiration, and only served to deepen her sense of gloom.

The queue moved excruciatingly slowly. Why did this bother her? she wondered. After all, she had nothing else to do. Nothing... The word jangled round in her mind and seemed to ricochet off the inside of her skull. Her parents had moved to Spain last year to start their new life as retired people, and however hard she tried to keep in touch with her two sisters, she rarely received a response. She supposed that must be something to do with the fact that they were both quite a bit younger and were having fun at university. But it hurt. Over the years, she had put a lot of effort into helping them to grow up – giving them encouragement and plenty of sound advice.

She hadn't yet been able to face letting Mum and Dad know about her job situation. It was easy enough to keep the conversation going when they phoned, as they had plenty to talk about in their new life, and she carefully steered away any searching questions. They were trying to get her to join them at Christmas, but she kept giving excuses, and made a vague promise of spending longer with them in the spring instead.

A voice broke into her thoughts. 'Hi, Miranda! You on holiday?'

Taken by surprise, she mumbled 'Sort of.'

The owner of the voice whistled a Christmas tune, and strode out onto the street in his muddy boots, allowing a blast of chilly damp air to flow in before the door banged shut.

Miranda liked Malcolm, but she felt detached, and could not connect with him. He had a market garden a couple of miles away from the village, and seemed to be making a reasonable living from it. She had a fleeting urge to run after him. But what for? In her current state, what would she get from that? She bit her lip, and waited.

At last it was her turn in the queue.

'Thirty-five second-class stamps,' she said.

'Christmas ones?'

She nodded.

The transaction complete, she turned and left.

The acquisition of the stamps had not lifted her mood. Instead she felt worse. She realised that she did not want to tell any of the thirty-five people anything about what had happened and how she was feeling, and she began to view the whole exercise of writing Christmas cards as meaningless.

There was one good thing, though. She had enough in her savings to keep her going. If she were careful, it would last quite a long time.

'Maybe I should do a course in something,' she murmured. But immediately she squashed the idea as being hopeless. All the courses for that year would have started weeks earlier, and in any case she had no clue about what would interest her, or would be of any use.

She shivered. Her winter coat with its padded lining did not seem adequate this year. She supposed that this must be something to do with her current situation, as last year it had been fine.

Back in her house she hung up her coat and turned on the gas fire. Her compact dwelling, with its low ceilings and its position sandwiched between others, was easy to heat, and for this she was very grateful. She shivered again, and turned the flames up high until the room felt comfortable.

'Maybe I should try to eat more?' she questioned. If she were honest with herself, she knew that she had been losing weight. She had adapted some of her clothes, but others just hung off her, and she had discarded them, at least for the time being.

She was startled when the phone began to ring. She st⌐

at it for a moment, and then answered it, but there was no one there.

As she sat and contemplated her position, one thing became very clear to her. Even if there was no immediate urgency to earn money, it was imperative that she involved herself in something… anything… soon. Through the weeks of working her notice, she had shunned her friends, and had stopped her usual evening activities. At the time this had seemed the natural thing to do, but now she could see that it had not been wise. In fact, it had been ridiculous! How could she have been so stupid? She glanced at her watch. The next bus to Branton would be coming in less than ten minutes. She could go to the Job Centre, phone Kate to see if she wanted to meet for lunch, and perhaps call in on June in the afternoon.

She grabbed her mobile and put it in her bag, turned off the fire, took an ageing banana from the fruit bowl, and put on her coat. Moments later she was out on the street again, jogging towards the bus stop.

As she had half expected, the Job Centre did not yield anything of long-term interest, but she was surprised to find that there was a range of part-time and sessional work, some of which almost attracted her. She took some time browsing, and eventually jotted some details in the notebook that she kept in her bag.

'Maybe I should try something completely different for a while,' she said aloud.

A familiar voice joined in from behind her. 'Me, too!'

Surprised, Miranda spun round to find Kate smiling at her.

'Fancy lunch?' asked Kate.

'I was about to phone you,' Miranda replied, laughing. 'What on earth are you doing here?'

'A letter was waiting for me on my desk when I got into work this morning,' Kate explained.

'Oh …' said Miranda, understanding straight away.

Kate went on. 'I thought I'd take a long lunch break to

organise my thoughts.'

'Let's get some soup at that new café on the corner of North Street,' Miranda suggested.

'Can't wait!' Kate replied. As they walked along together, she added, 'I might not have to slog through all of the four weeks' notice because I've got some holiday left. I'll see what I can fix up. It's going to be so depressing stuck at that desk.'

They found a table in the corner of the café, draped their coats on the seats, and went to collect soup and rolls from the counter.

When they were settled, Kate said bluntly, 'Miranda, I've been worried about you. I knew you were losing weight, and whenever I phoned in the evenings, there was no reply.'

'I think I must have been in a funny state,' Miranda acknowledged. 'I cut myself off from everything. I began to realise today that something was very wrong, and that's why I came into town.'

'Well, if it had gone on much longer, you would have had me hammering at your door,' Kate assured her.

Miranda smiled across the table to her friend. She had known Kate for a couple of years, and they had always got on well together. They had met through work. At first they were in different sections, but then Miranda was moved to the same one as Kate, and their desks had then been next to each other. Kate was outgoing and vivacious. She was younger than Miranda, but only by a few months. The friends were about the same height and build, but Kate had dark hair and dark brown eyes, whereas Miranda's hair was light brown, and her eyes were an unusual blue-grey. Miranda tended to be quieter than Kate, and more reflective, but when they were together, Miranda frequently talked as much as Kate did, if not more.

'We'll have to feed you up!' Kate remarked.

'I've made a start already,' Miranda replied as she produced the banana from her bag.

'I must get another job quite soon,' Kate confided. 'I used nearly all my savings when I bought my flat last year.'

5

'I've a bit of leeway,' said Miranda, 'and I've decided I'm going to think about a change of direction, although I haven't any clues yet.'

'Good for you,' Kate encouraged. 'What took your interest when you were in the Job Centre? I saw you scribbling furiously.'

'Nothing long-term.' Miranda felt embarrassed. She had wanted to keep her ideas to herself for now.

'Come on, spill the beans!' Kate urged, nudging her friend's foot under the table.

'Support worker or care worker. Dog walking. I just wanted something to do while I was thinking,' Miranda added hurriedly.

'Sounds fine to me. You'll meet some different people. Who knows, I might join you in a few weeks.' Kate hooted with laughter and pronounced, 'Here come Miranda and Kate with bunches of dog leads in each hand! I'd be fine because we always had dogs at home. How about you?'

'We didn't, but I used to look after the dog when the next-door neighbour was away. I might have to do some kind of course to be a care worker, but I'll look into it.'

Kate glanced at her watch. 'Drat! I'll have to get back to work. I don't feel like going, but it wouldn't be sensible to create a bad impression just when I'm needing a good reference.' She winked at Miranda, gave her a hug, and dashed off.

Miranda lingered on. She felt hungry, and not only did she finish her own food, but also she took the half roll that Kate had left, and plucked pieces off it – popping them mechanically into her mouth until nothing was left. She had no intention of going home yet. She searched her bag until she found her mobile phone. She selected a number and listened while it rang, but there was no reply. She was about to put it back in her bag when she thought better of it and tried the number again. This time it connected, but all she could hear was the very loud unmistakeable sound of a baby crying, and it sounded as if it were right next to the phone. She waited. June must surely be there…

Then she heard June's voice. 'Miranda? Can I phone you back in a few minutes? I'm trying to get Amy down for her sleep. She's exhausted.'

'Okay,' Miranda replied, raising her voice to ensure that June heard her.

Miranda bought a flapjack at the counter, and spent the next ten minutes absentmindedly crumbling it into her empty soup bowl, and then spooning it into her mouth.

June was on maternity leave, but Miranda had a strong feeling that she would not return to her full-time job. She was not sure how June and Simon would manage financially, but they were both very resourceful people, and she had no doubt that they would come up with a viable plan.

Her phone rang.

June's voice was calm. 'Sorry about that. Amy's asleep now. Where are you?'

'I'm in town, and I was wondering if I could come round for an hour.'

'That would be great!' June replied enthusiastically. 'You can stay as long as you like. Amy's got a bit of a cold. I went to the supermarket for a few things this morning, and I'm not going out again.'

'I'll be with you in about fifteen minutes,' Miranda promised. She rang off, grabbed her coat, and began to make her way in the direction of the street where June lived. She had known June since high school days. Even then June had known that she wanted to have a family, and by the time they left school, June had met Simon, and they had married by the time they were twenty. At first, they had lived with Simon's parents, who had a spacious house. It was not long before June confided that she was hoping to become pregnant quite soon. Miranda remembered the excitement in her voice that had accompanied the sharing of this information. But months passed, and then years, and eventually June and Simon went for fertility testing, which revealed that June's tubes were not in good condition, and no one could work out what had caused this. She remembered the day when June had told her. June had been distraught, as she and Simon had been told that the only option open to them was IVF. After much heart-searching they had decided against going ahead with that, and instead they continued to believe that it might be possible to conceive naturally. Their perseverance had been rewarded last year, when June missed a period and then found that she was pregnant. After that, everything had gone perfectly, and Amy had been born just one day after she was due.

Miranda reached the modern estate where June lived, and was soon at the door of her semi-detached house, tapping on it gently to avoid waking Amy. June opened the door straight away, welcoming her in with a big hug. Her frizzy red hair seemed to stick out even more than Miranda remembered.

'You're really thin!' June exclaimed worriedly. 'What's happened? You looked fine when you came to see me and Amy in hospital.'

'I was made redundant a month ago,' Miranda explained. 'I think I had such a shock that I forgot to eat.'

'That's terrible! I wish I'd known. You should have phoned. I've been so wrapped up in Amy. I think I assumed that because everything was working out for me, everyone else was fine.'

'Don't worry,' Miranda reassured her. 'I'm eating again now. I came into town today to look in the Job Centre, and I bumped into Kate from work. She heard this morning that she's losing her job, too.'

'I'm sorry to hear that.'

'Let's not talk about it now. June, it's good to see you looking so relaxed and well.' Although Miranda knew that June must be tired, she actually looked better than she had for years. She smiled and added, 'Motherhood suits you.'

'It's what I've always wanted,' June confirmed quietly.

'I know. You were always so certain. It's never been like

that for me.'

June gave her a penetrating stare, and opened her mouth as if to say something, but then shut it again.

'What were you going to say?' asked Miranda curiously.

'Nothing really.'

'Go on. Tell me.'

'Since I've had Amy, I've found myself thinking quite a lot about you and your sisters.'

Miranda was puzzled. 'Why? What do you mean?'

'There's only a year between them.'

'Yes, but Mum managed fine, because I helped a lot.'

June looked at her meaningfully. 'Exactly.'

'What do you mean "exactly"?'

'Your mum managed because you were there, and your sisters learned to rely on you. I've seen how they relate to you – they pick you up and put you down again just when it pleases them.'

Miranda opened her mouth to object, but she realised that what her friend had said was true.

June went on. 'They've treated you like most teenagers treat their parents. Oh, I know you wanted to help your mum, but the whole thing has left you in the position where you can't begin to think about whether or not you want a family of your own.'

Miranda gaped at her. 'I'd never thought about it like that before.'

'Well, I'm not going to go on about it,' June assured her. 'I just wanted you to know I'd been thinking about you.'

'Thanks.' Miranda fell silent.

Then June said, 'I'm thirsty. I'm going to put the kettle on. Would you like something?'

Miranda nodded. 'Yes, please.'

As they sat sipping their hot drinks, Miranda took a deep breath and confided, 'I haven't told my parents yet.'

'Why ever not?'

'I don't know. I've been avoiding telling them anything

about me and my life, but I haven't a clue why.'

'But they would want to know,' June pointed out firmly.

'I can see that. Anyway, things have changed today, and I'll tell them soon. In fact, I'm thinking of going out to visit them,' Miranda added decisively.

'I think that's a very good idea.'

'June… This may sound silly, but…'

'But what? Go on, tell me.'

Miranda hesitated.

'Tell me,' June urged.

'I think I'd like to learn how to do flamenco dancing.' Miranda blushed and put her hands on her cheeks in an attempt to hide their colour.

June could not conceal her astonishment. 'Flamenco dancing…' she repeated, savouring the idea.

Miranda's embarrassment melted away. 'Yes, flamenco dancing,' she said, surprised at the confidence that surged into her voice. 'I've wanted to try it since I was about fourteen. I saw some on television, and I knew it was for me, but I didn't know of anywhere that taught it.'

Back at home that evening, Miranda was taking her coat off when the phone began to ring.

'Bother!' she exclaimed. Her time with June had given her so much to think about that she had been looking forward to a couple of hours of pottering quietly, turning things over in her mind before she went to bed.

She glared at the phone rebelliously. Then she changed her mind and grabbed it, but it was too late. A moment later it rang again, and this time she answered it straight away.

She heard her mother's voice. 'Hello dear. I've phoned to see how you are. I thought the last time we spoke you sounded a bit down.'

'Oh, Mum…' A lump came into Miranda's throat, preventing her from continuing.

'Take your time, dear,' her mother advised.

'I've… I've been made redundant.'

'What happened?'

Miranda found that speaking about it was far easier than she had imagined, and she told her mother everything.

'With the financial climate as it is, this comes as no surprise,' her mother told her. 'And because you were in the first round of redundancies, you've probably felt especially bad.'

Miranda felt her body begin to relax.

Her mother continued. 'I only wish that you'd been able to tell us straight away.'

'Now I'm speaking to you about it, I wish that, too,' replied Miranda, 'but the whole thing seemed totally impossible before.'

'Miranda, do you need money?'

'I've got enough savings to tide me over for quite a while.'

'Well, you *must* let us know if you think you might get into difficulties,' her mother insisted.

'Thanks, Mum.'

'Never hesitate. Your dad and I both feel that your sisters are having more from us than you ever did…'

Here Miranda interrupted. 'But it's for their education.'

'I know, but it doesn't mean it's all right for you to end up with less.'

Miranda considered this. It was something that she had not thought about before. Amber had been born when her mother was forty, and Jessica when she was forty-one. Miranda herself was not quite six years old at Amber's birth. Right from when her sisters started school, Miranda had had the success of their education in the forefront of her mind. She had been so proud of them when they got their places at university.

'Did you hear me?' her mother asked.

'Yes, you were telling me to get in touch if I needed money.'

'Miranda, I thought you'd drifted off, and I was right. I was asking if you'd considered doing some full-time studying.'

Miranda was alarmed. 'Oh, I couldn't afford to do that!'

'Listen, dear, and I'll go through it again.'

'Okay.'

'I was telling you that your dad and I put some money aside a couple of years ago in case you needed it for further education. You don't have to make a decision about it now. I just want you to know it's there.'

Miranda felt flustered and confused. 'Er...'

'I think you probably need some time to think about it, so I'll ring off now, dear. I'll phone you again tomorrow evening. This is a difficult time for you, and I want you to be sure that you have our support.'

'Thanks, Mum,' Miranda whispered weakly. She heard a click as her mother put the phone down.

Miranda leaned back in her chair. She was glad that she was already sitting down, as she felt quite unsteady. It had been a big day for her. She had learned that Kate was heading in the same direction as herself. Now she had learned that for years her parents had been thinking about her future. Her mind whirled. So she wasn't alone after all. Yet over the last few weeks she had felt very alone indeed. And now, when she thought more about that feeling, she realised it wasn't a new one. But surely that couldn't be the case... She had never been alone. After all, she had always been part of a close, loving family... Maybe she'd felt her parents' move to Spain more than she had admitted to herself. But deep down she knew that the feeling had been around long before then.

The phone rang again.

Miranda picked it up and recognised Kate's voice straight away. 'Hi! It's me. I've some great news!'

'A job?'

'No such luck. But I've got new neighbours – Salma and Kareen. They're doing a flatshare and they're really nice. Are you free on Wednesday evening? We could ask them out.'

'Er... Yes... Yes, of course.'

'How about the Filmhouse? We could get something to eat

there first.'

Miranda quickly warmed to the idea. 'I'd like that. I'll put it in my diary. I…'

'What?'

'Actually I'd like to go even if they can't manage that evening.'

Kate chuckled. 'That's exactly what I was thinking, too.'

Miranda's stomach rumbled loudly as she put the phone down. She made something to eat, and found that she enjoyed every mouthful.

After she had finished, she searched her bookshelves and came across a book she had begun not long before she got the news of her redundancy. But as she settled herself to read, her mind drifted back to the conversation she had had with June that afternoon. There was something in it that had had an impact on her. What was it? Ah! Now she remembered. June had said something very perceptive about her relationship with Amber and Jessica.

And then a slow smile spread across her face as she remembered the way June looked when she had confided her wish to learn flamenco dancing. And maybe she should talk to her mother about firming up some dates for a visit to her parents' new home. Then she opened her book, and picked up where she had left off all those weeks ago.

Chapter Two

The next morning, Miranda woke with more energy than she had felt for months. She searched for her jogging clothes, and was soon heading towards the long tree-break at the edge of the village. It was barely light, and the air was fresh and frosty.

Back at home, she felt invigorated. She had a warm shower, and then cooked porridge for herself. Maybe she should do a little research about possible courses of study. But how could she do that when she had no idea what direction she wanted to take? 'Never mind,' she said aloud, 'I'll see what there is.'

An internet search of local college and university websites provided her with a wide and intriguing range of options. It felt surprisingly freeing to go through this exercise with no particular objective or plan, and she began to consider the possibility that although her job had provided a reasonable income and good companionship, it had not led to the kind of stimulation she really needed. She could not go as far as to say that the redundancy had been a blessing in disguise, but perhaps the saying 'every cloud has a silver lining' could be applied. Well, one thing was certain, she was going to do her best to ensure that something good came from all this. She spent the afternoon writing some of her Christmas cards, conveying that sentiment with her news. She then made a trip to the supermarket to stock up on appetising foods, while looking forward to the evening's phone call from her mother.

When the phone rang, Miranda was surprised to hear her father's voice.

'Your mother told me your news,' he began. 'I'll hand you over to her in a moment, but first I wanted to say we'll do all we can to help you.'

Miranda felt warmed by her father's unmistakeable support. She had always known that he was committed to the family, but if she were to be honest with herself, she had sometimes wondered if he had noticed her as much as her boisterous sisters.

'Thanks, Dad,' she said.

'We must keep in close contact,' he told her seriously.

Miranda didn't know what to say. His obvious concern was almost too much for her, and she was rather relieved when he said, 'I'll pass the phone across now.'

Miranda found that she was now eager to engage in conversation, and she spontaneously told her mother about the proposed outing with Kate and her new friends. She then went on to talk about her recent visit to see June and Amy.

When she put the phone down, the feeling of closeness that she had experienced during the call did not fade. Instead, she felt something inside her that was the emotional equivalent of the warmth that radiates from a glowing fire.

As she began to prepare her evening meal, the music of a song came into her head, but try as she might, she could not remember the words, or where she had heard it.

As she ate, it was almost as if there were people with her, eating, sharing confidences and laughing together, and she realised that it was a long time since she had felt like this.

When she went to bed, she read some more of her book. After that she slept soundly.

The following morning she got up early, and after jogging again along the tree break, she contemplated the day ahead. Although she had no plans until the evening, the hours ahead felt full of promise.

'I'll go through my wardrobe,' she announced aloud. 'I need to find something nice to wear.'

She rummaged through the altered clothes. Although there were things that would do for the occasion, she had an unfamiliar feeling of dissatisfaction about them.

15

'What do I *really* want to wear?' She laughed at herself. The person she had addressed was neither herself, nor a friend whom she imagined was there. How strange...

Then she ran lightly down the stairs, took a large jotter from the bookshelves, and opened its first blank page. To her delight, her mind filled with a picture of a longish dress of material that was covered with a glorious jumble of bright colours. She picked up a soft pencil, and found herself sketching a dress with a scooped neckline, three-quarter sleeves, and a close-fitting waist. This, made with the wonderful material, would be perfect! But maybe tonight she was going to have to settle for jeans and a plain top. An inner lurch of rebellion told her that this would not be acceptable, and she ran upstairs again to examine the contents of her jewellery box.

She spread everything carefully on her bed. There was the string of amber beads of varying shapes and sizes that Amber and Jessica had given her on her eighteenth birthday. She stroked the beads for a little while before putting them back in the box. There was the silver necklet with the jade pendant... No, not that.

One by one she contemplated the pieces and returned them to their box until only one item remained – her grandmother's pearls. Her mother's mother – Granny Ann – had been the best granny one could ever hope to have. And she hadn't had to share her. Although Granny Ann had grandsons, Miranda had been the only granddaughter. Her mind filled with happy memories of the many things that they had enjoyed together until... until the day when Granny Ann fell down the stairs and broke her hip. She didn't live much longer. The shock had been too much for her. Not long after that Amber was born, and everyone was taken up with looking after her.

Granny Ann had lived a very exciting life. She had not married until she was nearly forty, and all the years until then had been spent travelling round the world as a kind of carer-governess for sick children of families who were stationed abroad. Every evening, Granny Ann would have a different story to tell, and each story was fascinating. Miranda often wished that some of them had been written down. But how could she have known that Granny Ann would not be there forever?

Granny Ann had been given the pearls by a secret admirer. She had been willing to divulge this much, but nothing else. To this day Miranda had never been able to understand why her grandmother had consistently refused to reveal his identity. She had been so open about everything else, so why not this? When Miranda had pressed her, a closed look would come across her face, and she would talk about something else.

Miranda nestled the pearls lovingly into a corner of the box, right up against the rich purple velvet lining. 'Not tonight,' she whispered, selecting instead a silver chain that had the letters of her name interspersed between its links. She returned the box to its place on the chest of drawers beside her bed.

The evening out was great! Kate's new friends were such good fun. Salma had arrived in a stunning outfit – full-length tie-dyed loosely-fitting trousers with a matching waistcoat – that went well with her long black hair and dark skin. Kareen wore a skinny black top and tight black jeans that suited her figure perfectly. Kate was wearing a modest dress with a pair of her outlandish earrings. Kate's earrings were always a talking point. She had made a habit of adding to her collection whenever she had gone on holiday abroad, and the styles and materials were extremely varied.

They chatted and laughed together through the meal. Each had chosen a different dish, and they shared the food. The film was not particularly good, but before they parted, they talked about meeting again before Christmas as they had enjoyed themselves so much.

Miranda arrived home with a feeling of healthy tiredness. Again she recognised that this was something that she had not felt for a long time.

As she got into bed that night, she was almost certain that

the redundancy had not been a bad thing at all. It was helping her to take necessary steps that she might have avoided for a long time.

Chapter Three

'Guess what?' said Kate cheerfully when she phoned Miranda on Saturday morning.

'What's happened?'

Kate chuckled. 'Salma's got a man.'

'A man?'

'Yes, a man.'

'How did you find out?'

'Kareen came and knocked on my door late last night.' Kate chuckled again. 'She asked if she could put her sleeping bag on my floor and stay the night.'

'Did you let her?'

'I didn't feel I could refuse. She looked really fed up, and she had her sleeping bag under her arm, so I took pity on her.'

'I don't think it was very nice of Salma to cause that much trouble,' said Miranda slowly.

'Oh, it was fine. We sat up talking for a while, and then we went to sleep. Kareen's off to tackle Salma now though. I don't think she's going to put up with that again. After all, she's paying for half the flat. Between you and me, I think Salma's come from quite a restrictive family, and she's trying to spread her wings.'

'It's fine to spread wings so long as your feathers don't cascade over everyone else and stop them from breathing,' Miranda observed.

'That's a very good way of putting it,' said Kate. 'If I'm asked to contribute, I think I'll quote you. Hang on, that's someone at the door now.'

Miranda waited. She could hear raised voices. Then Kate came back on the phone.

'It's Salma and Kareen. Salma's in a bit of a state, and

Kareen is furious with her. I'd like to help them. Can I phone you back in a while?'

'Of course.'

It was well over an hour later by the time Kate phoned again.

'You've been ages,' Miranda remarked.

'Phew! What a mess,' said Kate. 'I hope I haven't held you up.'

'Don't worry about that. Just tell me what happened.'

'Well, for a start, I've sent Salma off for the morning-after pill.'

'Oh no!'

'Yes,' said Kate grimly. 'I told her she'd been watching too many films where people go straight into high-drama sex and seem to end up unscathed. Once she's back, I'll make her think about getting herself checked for Chlamydia... *and* everything else. Do you know, she'd only met him a couple of hours before,' she added crossly.

'You'd think that everyone would know how to take care of themselves nowadays,' Miranda commented. 'Years ago, when Amber and Jessica started looking at boys, I sat them down and put them in the picture.'

'Lucky people.'

'I asked them if they would ever lend their mobile phones to someone they didn't know well. They were really annoyed with me for asking, and said, "Don't be stupid, of course we wouldn't." So I said, "Well then, don't offer your body to anyone you don't know well." They both went really quiet for a while after that.'

Kate burst out laughing and couldn't stop. When eventually she managed to catch her breath, she asked, 'Did it work?'

'Yes.'

'Lucky, lucky people.'

'What exactly do you mean?'

'Just think about it. How many people have an older sister who would do that for them?'

'It's obvious. Who wouldn't do the same?'

'Sadly, there are many people who don't do that for their daughters or their younger sisters, and that's why so many people get themselves into a mess. Amber and Jessica are so lucky. I bet they're having a high old time at uni, but they know how to make sure they're safe. And by the way, I've just found out that Salma and Kareen are not a lot older than your sisters.'

'I miss Amber and Jess,' Miranda reflected. 'I really miss them.'

'Why don't you invite them for a weekend?'

Miranda fell silent for a moment, and then said sadly, 'I don't think they'd come.'

'You should ask them anyway.'

'Um...'

'What is it?'

'Er... If they said no, I'd be really upset.'

'It's silly to let that get in the way of asking them. Anyway, they might say yes. Tell you what, if they say no, we'll have a weekend together instead.'

Miranda could see the sense in what Kate had suggested. 'Hey, thanks for that. I'll text them soon. And... I don't want a weekend with you to be the fallback position. How about planning something anyway?'

'You're one step ahead of me. Yes, let's. I'll finish sorting these two out, and then we can hatch a plan.'

'No, let's start hatching now. There's no need for us to wait until Salma and Kareen are sorted out,' Miranda stated briskly.

'I like the sound of that. I can give them a bit of help, but they've got to find their own way. I don't want to end up parenting them.'

'That's right. We want them as friends.' Miranda paused for a moment before adding, 'And if Amber and Jess do come to visit, I'm not going to be looking after them.'

'Sounds good.'

'But if you see me sliding into it, give me a shake.'

Kate laughed. 'By the sound of you right now, I won't need

to.'

'Do you happen to be free this evening?' asked Miranda tentatively.

'As a matter of fact, I am. What have you got in mind?'

'Would you like to come over?'

'Mm… Thanks, I'd like that.'

'There's plenty to talk about.'

Kate's voice became serious. 'I don't like to admit this, but actually I'm starting to panic about work… and money.'

'I'm really glad you said that. I'm certainly willing to get on with talking about where we're heading – and not just the weekend away. Bring your night things in case you decide to stay over. We can cook something special for ourselves. I'll get a few surprise ingredients in.'

'Oh, thanks. That's really kind of you. I'll look forward to it.'

The morning seemed to rush past. Miranda put more thought into the idea of sending a text to Amber and Jess, but in the end she decided to put it off. Realistically, they would not want to come this month, so late January would be the earliest, and she did not know what she herself would be doing then, or where she might be.

She wondered about letting them know she was between jobs, but she decided against that, too, for now. The conversation with June, and now the one with Kate, had left her feeling uncertain about her relationship with her sisters, and she began to feel that she'd rather not be in touch with them until she was clearer about herself. That way she was more likely to relate to them as sisters, and not as if she were an extra parent to them.

When the post came, she found amongst the circulars an envelope containing a lovely card from her parents. Inside was a message that confirmed their promise to do all they could to help her. She felt tears well up in her eyes as she read and reread that message, and she looked forward with eagerness to their next conversation, which they had planned for Sunday evening.

She put the card in the centre of her small dining table, and was about to tear up the envelope when she realised that there was something else inside it. She took out the slip of paper that she found there, and read what was written on it. Her father had arranged his writing in a similar way to a cheque, and her mother had decorated it with designs like watermarks. It was a guarantee of financial support for two years in full-time study.

Miranda did not know whether she was laughing or crying, but realised that it must be both at the same time. Of course she had heard what they had said on the phone about having put money aside for her education, but the full impact of it had only just got through to her.

Suddenly she felt eager to continue writing her Christmas cards. Aware of the need to conserve global resources, she sent cards only to people who lived far away. Each had a dual purpose – a Christmas greeting, and a letter of news to keep in touch. She took out her writing pad, and began a letter to Rowan, an old school friend. An hour and several pages later, she signed the letter, chose a card, and addressed the envelope. That had felt good – as if once again she were chatting to her friend. She looked forward to a reply. Rowan had always been a bit scatty, and even now, she left writing her cards to the last possible day, so she would have Miranda's letter well before then. She wrote several more letters to go with cards, leaving only five more to write later.

Next, she browsed through her favourite cookery book, choosing an unusual recipe that would take a little while to prepare. She and Kate could have fun with it that evening, so long as she could find all the ingredients before then. She decided to do her shopping now, before dark, and continue writing cards and letters on her return.

Kate arrived soon after six o'clock. She dropped her overnight bag on the floor and gave Miranda a warm hug.

'This is such a great idea!' she exclaimed. 'I needed to get away from the drama so that I could concentrate on myself a bit, and your offer was perfect.' She bent down and unzipped her bag. 'I put some goodies in here. Look.' She produced a bottle of organic russet apple juice. 'I'm right into local produce these days, and this was bottled less than fifty miles away. I'm keen for you to try it. And I've made some spicy biscuits for us to nibble later on.'

'Thanks. That's lovely. And I've chosen a main course recipe and have bought everything we need for it.'

'Oh, let me have a look.'

Miranda pointed to the open book on the worktop.

Kate studied the illustration. 'It looks delicious. I'm hungry. Can we make a start?'

They enjoyed creating their meal together, and before eating, Kate took her mobile out of her bag, and took a photograph.

'I've got to keep a record of this,' she said proudly. 'We can eat at mine next. Hey, we can build up a repertoire! Eating out is all very well, but it costs a lot, and you can never be sure quite where things have come from. And it's such good fun making something together.'

Miranda smiled happily. Not long ago, everything had seemed very grim, but now she felt that there was warmth in her life, and she looked forward to planning her future.

'Kate,' she began. 'I've had a good piece of news today.'

'I'm glad. Tell me what it is.'

Miranda did not know quite how to put it to her friend, as she knew that Kate's current situation was far different from her own, but it would have felt wrong to keep it from her.

'Mum and Dad have put money aside in case I want to do some full-time studying.'

'Wow! That's wonderful news. Do you think you will?'

'I don't know yet. At the moment I'm just trying to get used to the idea that I've got it as an option. Apparently they would fund me for up to two years.'

Kate's response was spontaneous and genuine. 'Miranda, I'm so pleased for you.' She paused for a moment, and then added carefully, 'There's something I want to say, but I don't want you to pick me up wrongly.'

Miranda was curious. She leaned forward in her chair attentively. 'Go ahead.'

'I've always wondered why you were in a job where you didn't have to use your intelligence.'

Miranda opened her mouth to say something, but shut it again to let her friend continue.

'My attitude towards work has been different from yours. What I did was adequate, but I was never particularly devoted to it. I only wanted something to bring in the cash so that I could go off and have nice times out of work – evenings out, weekends and holidays.'

'I don't think I could say I was devoted to my work,' Miranda objected.

'In comparison with me, you were,' Kate insisted. 'You always put a bit extra into everything. You never made an issue of it. You just did it.'

Miranda stared at her friend. She struggled as she tried to take in what she had said. 'Mm... I'll have to think about that.'

'Miranda, it's the way you are with everything. I think that you were undervalued at work, and at worst, used. People assumed that you would always give that extra bit, but you got no credit for it. It wasn't right. I'm not happy about the way you were made redundant, but I'm really glad you don't work there any more.' Kate paused for breath, and then ended by saying, 'I think you're destined for higher things.'

'Kate, it's kind of you to say all that.' Miranda smiled across at her friend. 'I don't know if I'll be able to live up to your aspirations, but I'll try,' she added earnestly. 'But we should be talking about you as well. You said on the phone that you were worried about work and money. Where do you want to start?'

Kate groaned.. 'I don't know... I just don't know. One

thing's for sure. I need an income.'

'Most of us do,' Miranda agreed, 'but it seems that I'm lucky enough to be in the position where I've got some breathing space.'

'I've got very little – a couple of months, perhaps three at a push. Even if I get some part-time or temporary work, I'll be struggling.'

Miranda noticed that Kate looked quite pale, and her usual cheerful demeanour had gone. She searched her mind for something helpful to say. Then an idea occurred to her.

'Kate,' she began tentatively, 'I've thought of something.'

'Any ideas are welcome,' Kate replied in a voice that was devoid of emotion. 'I've run out of them – at least for now.' She took a deep breath before continuing. 'I might have to sell my flat. The market's not good at the moment, but it might pick up a bit by the time I have to make a decision.'

Miranda hesitated for only a fraction of a second before saying, 'Well then, my idea might come in handy.'

Kate looked at Miranda and waited.

Miranda continued. 'You could let your flat.'

'I'd thought of that. But I wouldn't have anywhere to live.'

'You can live here, with me.'

'I couldn't possibly do that.'

'Why not?'

'Well… It's your home. It's just the right size for you.'

'I know it's not all that big, but we could manage,' Miranda assured her. 'We could find a way.'

Kate stared at her. 'You really mean it, don't you?'

Miranda nodded emphatically. 'Of course I mean it.'

'But wouldn't you get fed up – tripping over me and my things all the time?'

Miranda laughed. 'Come upstairs and I'll show you something.'

Curious, Kate followed her, and she watched as Miranda collected a long pole from her bedroom, and stood under a hatch on the small landing.

'Hey presto!' she said, as she released a catch and the hatch opened. A minute later, she had pulled down a ladder, and was climbing up it. 'Follow me,' she instructed.

Kate followed her obediently. Somewhere deep inside her she felt like a small child following a capable and competent leader, but her overriding feeling was one of hope about the insoluble dilemma in her life.

They stood together in the empty loft.

'I had no idea that this was here,' said Kate. She surveyed the contrast between the flawless laminate flooring, and the rough inside of the roof.

'I've never used it. The man who lived here before me was in the middle of converting it into a space for his hobbies. It's not a living or sleeping space, but it can be used for storage. If you're going to be living with me for a while, I'll put some of my things out of the way up here, and there'll be enough room for most of your belongings as well. Anyway, you can think about it.'

Kate hugged her friend impulsively. 'I'll try my best to avoid invading you, but if all else fails, I'll come. Thank you, thank you and thank you again.'

'It's okay,' said Miranda earnestly. 'I'm so lucky having savings and now this offer of help from my parents.' She knew that Kate's family could not help her. Her father had left when she was still at primary school, and her mother had had to get by on very little money. She had worked hard in several small jobs to keep things going, but it had been very difficult. Kate's older brother, Graham, had reacted very badly to his father abandoning them, and had had a long struggle with alcohol addiction, which at thirty-five, he was only now beginning to recover from. Miranda continued. 'I think you should be able to let your flat quite easily.'

'I thought that, too,' Kate agreed. 'Maybe in the end it'll work out being a good thing that I opted for something in town. I stretched myself when I got it, and with the present situation, I've wished I hadn't.'

'Well, you're not to worry about that any more,' Miranda said decisively. 'As far as I'm concerned, it's settled. You can move in with me any time after the New Year.'

'We'll have to talk about rent,' Kate pointed out.

'We can leave that for now.'

'I don't think we should. And I wouldn't feel comfortable about coming unless we had some kind of written agreement.'

Miranda said nothing, but began to descend the ladder. She felt puzzled, but by the time they were back in the living room, she could see what Kate meant.

'Okay,' she agreed. 'Something simple.' She picked up a notebook and began to jot some ideas down. 'I'd want you to have the first bit of time here as a guest. How about the first three months being rent-free, but sharing expenses?'

'That would be a huge help. But if having let my flat I then land a decent job, I'd want to pay rent to you straight away. And I think I should pay half of any council tax right from the beginning.'

Miranda thought about this. It seemed fair, so she did not argue, and added these ideas to her notes. Then she closed her notebook, stating firmly, 'We can work the rest out later.'

'One more thing,' Kate insisted. 'Being friends is one thing. Doing a house-share is quite another. What if it takes me a long time to get on my feet again? I don't think it would be right for me to be here more than say six months.'

'Why ever not?' asked Miranda.

'Think about it,' said Kate patiently. 'Six months is a long time to put your domestic life on hold.'

'But I wouldn't be. I would still have a domestic life. It would be a different one. That's all.'

'What if you wanted to invite Malcolm round for dinner?' asked Kate bluntly.

'Malcolm? Why would I want to ask him round?' Miranda wrinkled her nose. 'He's always covered in mud.'

Kate hooted with laughter. 'That needn't deter you. You could put newspapers down! No, seriously... What if you got interested in somebody, and wanted privacy?'

'I hadn't thought about that,' Miranda admitted. 'But the same would be true for you. What would happen then?'

'I'd eat out,' said Kate flatly. 'And I'd be celibate – unless whoever it was invited me back to his place. Anyway, I haven't got time or energy for that. I've got to straighten my life out first, and I'm not going to take any risks with people I don't know properly. I made my mistakes with that years ago. It's you I'd be concerned about. Seriously though, if you wanted a night without me here, you should tell me, and I'd fix something up.'

Miranda smiled. 'You're way ahead of me, but thanks anyway. Look, now we've got our worries about accommodation sorted out, we both need to think about our careers. To study or not to study is my dilemma. What's in your mind?'

'A mess,' Kate confessed. 'A big mess. I can see that I've been acting a bit too much like an overgrown adolescent, and I need to take some steps forward now. But I don't know how to go about it.'

'I don't think you've been acting like an adolescent. For instance, look at how you've been helping Salma and Kareen.'

'That's not what I mean,' said Kate patiently. 'It's more to do with work. Work takes up such a big part of life – getting ready to go, being there, and coming home again. But most of the time I'm there, I'm thinking about what I'm going to do when I get home.'

'That must be awful,' Miranda reflected.

'Yes, when I look at it now I can see that it is, but most of the time I'm pretending it's an okay way to go about things. And I drifted through school in much the same way. I could, because I've got enough intelligence to work out how to get by. But it's wrong... all wrong.'

Kate looked so miserable that Miranda leaned across and patted her hand saying, 'We're both going to have to change.'

'Probably me more than you,' said Kate dolefully.

'I don't agree!' Miranda retorted.

Miranda's response was so forceful that it jerked Kate out of her mournful state. 'What do you mean?'

'I'm finding it a huge challenge to face change. Kate, you were right when you said that I was undervalued at work. I would blind myself to it and do the best I could with each day. I'm beginning now to realise how unsatisfying that was. And the chance of more education is wonderful, but I'm scared stiff thinking about what direction to take.' Miranda leaned forward in her chair, and looked straight into her friend's eyes. 'Kate, have you *ever* had something in your mind that you really wanted to do?'

To her astonishment, Kate's eyes filled with tears.

'What is it?' Miranda asked, concerned.

'When I was at primary school, I knew that when I grew up I wanted to be a teacher.' Then she added in a whisper, 'Like Dad.'

Silently, Miranda stood up, fetched a box of tissues, and handed them to Kate. Then she waited.

Eventually Kate was able to continue. 'I thought my dad was wonderful, and I just couldn't believe it when he left. I used to go and see him, but he would never talk to me about why he had left. And when I was fourteen, he got together with someone else – someone who had a daughter about the same age as I had been when he left. He was really good with her, and the whole thing hurt so much that I couldn't bear going to see him any more. He thought I was being difficult. After that I only did enough studying to get by. Education wasn't for me any more.'

'Kate, I'm really glad you told me all this,' said Miranda gently.

'I was so ashamed of what happened that I didn't tell anyone about it, and how I felt.'

'There's quite a lot to think about,' Miranda reflected. 'I can see that it isn't just a question of working out what to choose for a way forward for each of us. We've each got painful feelings from the past that are getting in the way. What you've just told me explains a lot about you.'

'Yes, I can see that myself now. I could see so clearly how you had been affected by concentrating on what your sisters needed, but until now I couldn't see what had affected me.'

'We're so lucky to have each other as friends,' said Miranda suddenly. 'We can keep reminding each other of this conversation. It's bound to help us both.'

Kate smiled. 'I see what you mean, but there are times when I would prefer a magic wand.'

'Magic wouldn't really sort things out. It would only put off the day when we had to tackle things properly.'

'I'll settle for winning the lottery then.'

'The idea's tempting, but we've got to assume that's not going to happen,' said Miranda bluntly.

Kate became serious. 'Your offer of having me here has taken a huge load off my mind. Miranda, I'm so grateful. That, and seeing what happened to me after my dad left, might leave me more able to think straight about what to aim for now.'

'You'll probably need time to let it sink in. I'll certainly need time to let my parents' offer sink in before I'll be able to work out what to do with it.'

Just then the phone started to ring.

'I wonder who that is?' said Miranda as she picked it up.

Kate watched with amusement as Miranda looked first pleased, and then somewhat agonised. She held the phone several inches away from her ear, and Kate could hear a loud voice talking incessantly, although she could not make out what it was saying.

After a few minutes there was a pause, and Miranda managed to say, 'That's wonderful news, but could you slow down a bit?'

A sound akin to a loud cackle came down the phone, and Miranda winced. 'Hang on a minute, Tess, I've got someone with me. Can I explain to her what's going on?'

Miranda turned to Kate. 'It's Tess – a friend who used to

31

live on the same street when I was young. She's called to let me know she's getting married in the summer. She's so excited that I can hardly get a word in.'

'I can see that,' Kate replied dryly. 'I'm off to the bathroom. I'll let you get on with it.'

Kate took her time upstairs. She didn't feel enthusiastic about weddings at the moment. There was too much else that was occupying her mind. And if she were honest with herself, she had to admit that she would like to get together with someone, but every time she had tried, something had gone wrong, leaving her doubtful about whether she would ever find anyone. It was always the same. Just at the point when things could have become serious, she would start feeling terribly anxious, and would call a halt to the relationship.

Downstairs, she found Miranda doing what seemed to be a good job. She was asking questions that definitely sounded as if she were interested to hear the answers, and the interaction was more of a conversation than the one-sided blurting that it had been at the beginning.

Miranda glanced over her shoulder when she heard Kate return.

'Tess,' she said firmly, 'I'd love to hear the rest of it, but it'll have to wait for now. Are you free on Monday evening? ... Good ... Can I phone you around nine? ... Eight would be better? Yes, that would be fine for me. Bye for now.'

She replaced the handset. 'She's over the moon,' she explained unnecessarily.

'She sounded out of her box,' Kate commented irritably. 'Oh, I'm sorry! She's your friend.'

'I found it hard at the beginning,' Miranda admitted, 'but she's so excited that it's infectious.' She smiled indulgently. 'I think she's found someone who will suit her perfectly. From what I gathered, he can talk as fast as she can, he's got a secure job, they're buying a house together, and he's good fun. That's exactly what she needs. She wanted to tell me all about her dress and the wedding venue as well, but that will have to wait until Monday evening.'

'Spare me the details when we speak again,' begged Kate. 'I don't mean to be unkind, but I would prefer a summary.'

'Don't worry,' Miranda assured her. 'We've got more important things to discuss. But remember, when it's our turn, we might be glad of a friend like her.'

'Our turn?' Kate retorted indignantly. 'Exactly what do you mean?'

Miranda was startled by the sharpness of Kate's tone. 'As you know, I haven't got anyone, but I haven't ruled marriage out. Have you?'

Again Kate's eyes filled with tears. 'It's a sore point,' she confessed. 'Can we leave it for now?'

Miranda nodded and reached out to touch Kate's arm affectionately. 'Of course we can. Let's get ourselves something to nibble, and then we'll decide what to talk about next.'

'Perfect. We'll fatten you up a bit while planning your future.'

'I've got a bag of chestnuts. We could grill some,' Miranda suggested.

'Sounds good. I haven't had any for years. Mum used to put some at the front of the fire when I was small.' Kate laughed. 'Sometimes they exploded.'

Miranda slit the skins of the chestnuts and turned the grill on. 'I'll put it at medium. That should be safe enough.'

'Miranda, if you're going to apply for further education, now's the time to fill in the forms,' Kate pointed out.

'I know. It would make sense to start something next September, but the trouble is I haven't a clue what to go for. I've had a look to see what's on offer, but there's so much. I feel overwhelmed.'

'Have you thought about talking to a careers advisor?'

'Well... actually... no.'

'It wouldn't do any harm, and something might come out of it.'

'We could both go.'

'I don't think there's any point for me,' Kate replied. 'I can't take time out to study.'

'That might not be needed,' Miranda insisted. 'You never know. And there may be part-time courses that can be done in the evenings and at weekends.'

Kate pulled a face, but then became serious. 'You're right. I hadn't thought about it like that before.' She stood up as straight as she could, and announced, 'I must not leave any stone unturned.'

This left Miranda shaking with laughter.

Kate rescued the chestnuts as they were now in danger of burning, and they shared them out.

'Are you going to your parents at Christmas?' asked Kate as she tried to peel the first of hers.

'Most probably not. Why do you ask?'

'I was thinking of going to see my mum. She likes eating turkey with me. Want to come?'

Miranda considered this, and then asked, 'How would your mum feel about that? Wouldn't she prefer to have you to herself?'

'Not really. I think she'd like to meet you, and she likes having people round.'

'Where does she live?'

'Tronton. It's a couple of hours by train.'

'Where would we stay?'

'I take my camping mat and spread it out in the living room. You could do the same. She's got spare duvets and pillows. We'd have to stay for three nights because there won't be any trains on Christmas Day and Boxing Day.'

Miranda smiled. 'It's a nice idea. But will you check with her, and let me know what she says? Please don't put any pressure on her on my account.'

'Don't worry about that.'

Miranda yawned. 'I suddenly feel exhausted. Do you mind if we go to bed soon?'

34

'Of course not. I've been unwinding quite a lot this evening, and I could certainly do with some sleep now.'

Chapter Four

The Monday evening phone conversation with Tess turned out to be much more interesting than Miranda could have imagined. Contrary to her expectations, Tess was planning an unpretentious wedding ceremony at her local church, and Miranda was astonished to discover that she hoped to make her own dress.

'Yes,' Tess confirmed excitedly, 'I'm determined. I've been going to dressmaking classes, and I've learned a lot already. Once I've got the basics, a friend of Mum's will help me to choose a pattern that I'm bound to be able to manage, and she'll give me a hand whenever I need it. We're going to book a hall for the reception and have a buffet of healthy food. And...' she announced dramatically, 'there won't be any alcohol. Stevie and I are in complete agreement about that.'

Miranda was stunned. It seemed that Tess was changing very quickly. She remembered only too well how her friend had gone for years barely letting a day go by without buying a bottle of wine. She began to wonder if perhaps Stevie's family did not drink.

As if reading her thoughts, Tess went on. 'Of course Stevie would have been happy to have champagne, but I put my foot down, and he could see the sense in giving it a miss. After all, a marriage should not depend upon partying.'

Miranda struggled for words. 'Er... What you're planning sounds really nice.'

Tess rushed on. 'You'll be invited of course. I can't wait for you to meet Stevie. He's wonderful!'

'What's the date?' asked Miranda, feeling a little as if she were part of a dream. A Tess who was staying at home and sewing was a person she had never known before, and a Tess who had renounced alcohol seemed impossible to imagine. Yet it all seemed to be real.

'June 16th,' Tess replied, oblivious of Miranda's reaction. 'Stevie's great at DIY, so we want to find a house that needs a lot of work doing to it. He's going to teach me loads.'

'I'll put the date in my diary,' Miranda promised enthusiastically. 'And if you're doing a wedding present list, let me see it so that I can choose something to buy for you.'

'That's really kind of you. Stevie and I aren't expecting anything. What we want is to be surrounded by nice people on our wedding day, and that's the best present we could ever have.'

Miranda could tell that what Tess had said was entirely genuine. She was astonished and delighted by the changes in Tess' life, and she was already looking forward to being at the wedding. She and Tess talked for a while longer, and at the end of the call, they agreed to speak again in a few weeks' time.

'I expect you'll have more news by then, and I'll look forward to hearing it all,' said Miranda. 'I'm so impressed that you're going to be making your dress. You must tell me when you have finally decided on the design.'

'Thanks a lot,' Tess replied. 'And when we speak again, I want to find out what you've been up to. I'm hugely excited about my wedding plans, but I don't want that to get in the way of hearing your news, too.'

After the call, Miranda sat quietly for a while. How had Tess matured like this, and so quickly? She would probably never know the answer to these questions. Two other thoughts came into her mind. The first was that if Tess could change, then so could Amber and Jessica. The other was about that dress she had imagined last week. Maybe she could make it for herself?

Miranda was looking forward to Friday evening. Kate had insisted that she should go and stay the night with her. They had wondered about inviting Salma and Kareen to join them for the evening, but in the end decided against it. They needed the time to continue working out what they should do.

When Miranda arrived, Kate greeted her excitedly. 'Come in, come in. That's it fixed.'

Miranda was puzzled. 'What's fixed?'

'Christmas, of course. Mum was delighted when I said you might come with me. She told me to say that she's counting the days until we arrive.'

Miranda smiled. 'That's really nice.' There was a warm glow inside her as she took in the news.

'We'll put your bag in the bedroom, and then you can sit down and put your feet up. I've got everything under control.'

By this time, Miranda had become aware of an interesting aroma drifting through from the small kitchen. 'Smells wonderful, but I thought our cooking was a joint project.'

'Well, tonight it's a surprise,' said Kate as she put Miranda's bag away.

'By the way, the phone call with Tess went fine,' Miranda began.

'Judging by the deluge I overheard, I'm not sure I want to know anything else.'

'All I need to say is that I'll be going to the wedding in June, and I'm looking forward to talking to Tess again next month.'

A look of disbelief spread across Kate's face. 'Miranda, are you *sure*?'

'Of course I am. Kate, she's changed a lot. She's really matured.'

'It didn't sound like it when I was there,' Kate commented suspiciously.

'I think the best thing I can say is that it left me thinking if Tess can change like this, then so can Amber and Jessica.'

'Wow! Okay, I'll believe you about her, but always remember not to give me details.'

'I promise.' Miranda noticed that Kate was looking slightly pale.

'Um…'

Miranda waited.

'Er… I suppose I ought to say something about me and men.'

'You don't have to.'

'I do have to,' Kate stated quietly. She took a deep breath. 'I've been thinking a lot since I was at yours. To put it in a nutshell, I'm pretty sure that whenever I get close to someone, I start worrying that they're going to go away like Dad did, and so I end up going away first.'

'Do you mean that you got to the point with someone where you were thinking about living together?'

'Yes, that's right. Actually, it's happened more than once. It all seems fine until we start talking about finding somewhere to live together.'

'What happens?'

'I don't really know, but it always ends up that we go our separate ways.'

Miranda sensed that Kate had taken this subject as far as she could for the moment. She asked nothing further, but commented, 'No wonder you're edgy about weddings.'

'How about you?' asked Kate quickly.

'I haven't come across anyone I want to get that close to.'

Kate stared at her. 'Are you sure?' she asked incredulously.

Miranda nodded. 'It isn't that I don't like them. It's just that I like them as if they were brothers.'

'No passion…?'

Miranda shook her head.

'Oh…' Kate felt lost for words. Then she smiled. 'Hey, that means we've got two major puzzles to sort out – our employment and our love life. Could be fascinating!'

Miranda could see that the colour had come back into her friend's cheeks.

Then Kate leapt to her feet. 'I sense some overcooking might be taking place,' she announced, and rushed to the kitchen. 'Don't come,' she called. 'Everything's under control.

Well… sort of.'

Miranda picked up a magazine that was lying under a chair, and flipped through its pages. The main features looked uninspiring, but there were some shorter pieces that were quite interesting, and she soon became absorbed.

She was startled when Kate came back, carrying a tray on which there were two plates, each piled high with food.

'Wow!' Miranda exclaimed. 'That's impressive. But are you expecting me to get through one of these food mountains?'

'Yes, of course.' Kate grinned. 'You're supposed to be boosting your intake. Remember?'

Carefully examining the creation on her plate, Miranda found that it was made from several layers. The bottom one was rice, the next two were different mixtures of baked vegetables, and the top layer looked fresh and very green.

'Why not go ahead and eat it?' Kate prompted.

As Miranda selected from the layers, she found that each was flavoured in ways that caught her by surprise.

Kate watched her with some amusement.

Miranda was clearly impressed. 'I didn't know that you could do this sort of thing.'

'Well, actually, neither did I,' Kate informed her, 'but I decided to give it a bash.' She hesitated for a moment, and then the next thing she said came out in a rush. 'The last person who was nearly my life's partner used to make it. When I decided I wasn't going to be with him after all, I vowed I would never eat anything like this again.' She took a quick breath, and rushed on. 'But now I know something's got to change, and I thought this was as good a place to start as any.'

Miranda stared at her friend. She was aware that something profound was happening, and she didn't want to say anything that Kate might find unhelpful.

As if reading her mind, Kate continued. 'Don't worry, you can tell me I've been an idiot. I won't be offended.'

Miranda was horrified. 'I wouldn't say anything like that! You know I've got my own problems.'

'I think it's only that you've not met the right person yet, whereas I think I've met a lot of right people, and then look what I did.' Kate put her laden plate on the coffee table and looked very dejected.

'I don't agree. Each of us has a problem that we've got to get to the bottom of. Neither of us has done anyone any harm,' Miranda pointed out firmly.

'I'm not so sure. It can't have been very nice for my boyfriends to be dumped.'

Miranda was no longer concerned about whether or not to ask questions. 'Kate, what did you say to them?'

Her friend looked at her, surprised. 'Why do you ask?'

'Just tell me.'

'I'd say something about having had a great time together, but that I wasn't ready to settle down with anyone yet.'

Miranda gaped. 'But that's perfect!'

Kate thought for a while. 'I suppose it's not too bad,' she admitted, 'but I think that the speed at which I delivered it, and then grabbed my things and ran, must have been rather startling.'

At this, Miranda could not help laughing. She laughed so much that the food was in danger of sliding off her plate, and she put it on the coffee table beside Kate's. 'Oh,' she gasped, 'I've got a cartoon image in my mind of you rushing away with beads of sweat flying off you, and it's so funny.'

Kate began to see the funny side of it herself, and started to giggle.

Whenever one of them began to calm down, the other would break out afresh with hoots of laughter.

'And now I've got a ridiculous picture of me, too,' Miranda blurted out.

'Can't... wait... to... hear... it.'

'I see a potential man... and almost straight away I think of him as an untidy hairstyle, muddy feet, a long nose, or whatever. So my cartoon image is of me with a wonderful man, but I can't see him. All I see is what is in the thought bubbles over my head – full of long noses and all that.'

At this, Kate clutched at her sides, and she laughed until her face ached. 'What a pair we are!' she managed to say.

When their laughter eventually subsided, Kate picked up her plate. 'Cold,' she commented starkly.

'Well, I feel so warm with all that laughing, I prefer it like that,' Miranda replied, and she ate the rest of her food hungrily.

Kate finished hers more slowly. 'There's a bit left in the kitchen,' she said uncertainly.

Miranda jumped out of her chair. 'Great, I'll finish it up.' Then she stopped and added, 'Hope you don't mind.'

Kate shook her head with an amused expression. 'Fill up your waistband, Miranda. That's exactly what's needed.'

Miranda returned carrying a dish, and proceeded to scrape it out with a spoon.

'I like to see you making yourself at home,' Kate told her. 'And Mum will like that when we see her at Christmas, so don't be on your best behaviour.'

'I'm really looking forward to those days already. Kate…'

'I'm all ears.'

'We were right not to invite Salma and Kareen round. They're nice people, but we need time to ourselves. And I'm definitely not going to contact Amber and Jessica until I've sorted more out for myself.'

'I couldn't agree more.' Kate paused. 'Miranda…'

'Yes?'

'Are you still serious about your offer that I can stay with you for a while?'

Miranda nodded emphatically.

'Really serious?'

'Really, really serious.'

'Then…' Kate struggled. 'I'd like to take you up on it.'

'Wonderful!' Miranda reached out and grabbed Kate's hand tightly. 'It's the right decision,' she assured her.

'I've had a low-key chat with a letting agent, and I've been doing some sums,' Kate confided. 'If I'm living with you, I can survive for quite a long time while I'm trying to pull my life round.'

'It's going to be the best decision you've made for a long time,' said Miranda confidently. 'You'll see.'

As Miranda returned home the next day, she looked forward to phoning her parents later. The call hadn't been planned, but there was now a lot of news that she was eager to tell them. Christmas Day was at the end of next week, and by then she would be with Kate at her mother's house. She made a note on her shopping list to buy a large bag of chestnuts to take with her, and she would think of other things as well.

The rest of the day passed quickly as she began to go through her possessions, deciding which to pack away in the loft while Kate was living with her. The anticipation of their sharing her home gave her a cosy feeling, and she hummed a cheerful tune.

When she phoned her parents, it was her mother who answered.

'Oh, it's you, Miranda! What a lovely surprise.'

'I've got some good news,' Miranda told her excitedly. 'I'm going with Kate to stay with her mother over Christmas, and after that it won't be long before Kate will be moving in with me for a few months.'

'That's sounds really nice, dear.'

Miranda rushed on. 'Kate is having to look for other work, and she hasn't got much in savings, so we've planned that she can let out her flat and come and live with me for a while. We're both putting in a lot of thought about future work, and we'll be able to help each other with that.'

'I'll tell Dad your news. I'm sure he'll be just as pleased for you as I am. Now do remember, we'll be interested to hear how Kate is getting on, so keep us up to date about both of you.'

Miranda could hear the genuine warmth in her mother's voice, and she said, 'I'll let Kate know. She was a bit unsure about taking up my offer, and she's determined to contribute to all the costs. It'll mean a lot to her that you're thinking about her.'

Her mother continued. 'Of course, it would have been wonderful if you were here for Christmas. You're both welcome any time.'

'Maybe once we've sorted some things out we could come to see you,' Miranda suggested.

'As soon as you can give us dates, we'll have the beds ready,' her mother replied cheerfully.

Chapter Five

The afternoon of Christmas Eve saw Kate and Miranda waiting on the station for the train to Tronton. It was already nearly dark. When the train arrived, it was rather full, but they managed to squeeze past luggage that was overflowing into the corridor, and found seats not too far from each other. Miranda pulled a novel out of her bag, and was soon engrossed in the story. She had borrowed it from the library, although she had very little idea of what the content might be. She had merely picked one that a librarian had just returned to the shelves.

She lost all track of time as she turned the pages. It was the story of someone who had contracted TB in the 1930s, and what conventional treatment offered in those days. Clearly, the sufferer had had to face the kind of adversity that was unknown in the developed world now, but there was a message in this tale that was very relevant to any sufferer of a long-term intractable problem, and Miranda found this uplifting.

She was wrested out of her concentration when she heard Kate's voice in her ear.

'There's a seat free next to mine. I've put my coat and bag across them both, but come quickly.'

Miranda grabbed her things. For a moment, the whole scene appeared strange, so immersed had she been in the content of the book. Then she quickly remembered where she was and the purpose of the journey, and followed Kate.

'What are you reading?' asked Kate, as they settled themselves. 'I had to speak to you three times before you heard me. Is it a riveting story of world travel or something?'

'No, not at all. The main character is stuck in bed for months, with sandbags up against her so that she can't move.'

'You're joking!'

Miranda was indignant. 'No, I'm not.'

'Sorry. I didn't believe you because I couldn't imagine that you could have been so absorbed in that kind of story. What is it about it that grabs you?'

Miranda went on to explain. 'It's endurance in the face of extreme adversity. This woman never loses heart. That's what affects me.'

'I think I'm beginning to understand,' said Kate slowly. 'We think we're having a tough time, and we can't see how to surmount the problems we have, but there she is, completely at the mercy of that treatment, and somehow it never gets her down to the point where she wants to give up.'

'That must be why she lived to tell the tale. She survived TB in the 1930s, you know.'

'Is it a true story, then?'

'It's presented as a novel, but I'm certain it's a slice of real life as it was at the time.'

'What's the title?'

'The Plague and I.'

Kate drew in a breath. 'Pretty stark. But I think we can both put it to good use.'

'What do you mean?'

Kate looked directly at her friend. 'What I mean is that every time we feel stuck or defeated, we have to remember this.'

Miranda smiled. 'Yes, we can use it as a sort of prompt. "The Plague and I." Sounds good, doesn't it?'

Kate nodded vigorously. 'So when I'm thinking that I'll never be able to settle down with a man, you can say...'

'... The Plague and You!'

'Got it!'

At this, they laughed so much that passengers several rows down turned their heads to see what was happening.

When Miranda could speak again, she said, 'And when I'm in a blue funk about what course of study I should choose, you can say...'

'Remember the Plague!' Kate glanced at her watch. 'Oh!'

46

she exclaimed. 'All this hilarity made me forget the time. We must be nearly there.' She did her best to peer through the window, but it was very dirty, and there were only a few distant lights, so she could not see enough to be able to work out where they were. 'It's bound to be the next station,' she pronounced confidently. 'Come on, let's collect our things and stand next to a door.'

Ten minutes later they were standing on the draughty platform of Tronton station, and Miranda began to shiver.

'Let's get a taxi,' Kate suggested.

'How far is it to your mum's place?'

'About fifteen minutes' walk.'

'Let's go on foot. I need to move about a bit, and we haven't got all that much luggage. I'll soon warm up.'

'Okay,' Kate agreed cheerfully. 'This way.'

She set off at a brisk pace, and Miranda walked alongside her.

'Do you know what Salma and Kareen are up to?' Miranda asked.

'I think Salma's gone to stay with family, and Kareen's hoping to put her feet up and have a quiet time. How about June?'

'As far as I know, Simon's brother and wife and child are staying for a few days. I dropped off a little present for Amy. She's a bit young to know what's going on, but I liked choosing something for her.'

'What did you get?'

'A sort of musical mobile thing that you hang from the ceiling.'

'Sounds good. Could do with one myself for when I can't sleep,' Kate joked. 'Turn left here.'

Miranda stopped to turn up the collar of her coat, as the wind was by now very piercing.

'Only another street to go,' Kate encouraged.

'Actually, I'm enjoying this. After two hours on a crowded train, I'm glad to discover that I can move about freely,'

Miranda explained. 'Kate, what's your mother's place like?'

'You'll soon see. I'll keep it as a surprise,' Kate added with an air of mystery. 'Turn right here.'

As Miranda turned the corner on to the next road, she gasped. On each side of the tree-lined street were detached houses of considerable size. 'There must be some mistake. Surely you said we would be sleeping on the floor?'

'All will be revealed.'

Kate led the way down the drive of the third large house on the right, but instead of approaching its front door, she went down the side of it and into the garden behind.

It was dark, and Miranda began to feel nervous, but she followed her friend without saying anything further. Kate seemed to merge into the darkness, and Miranda felt panic rise in her throat until she heard her calling. Then she realised that Kate had gone round the side of a dense hedge. She joined her, and saw a tiny cottage with light shining from its front window.

'Mum loves it here,' Kate explained. 'She keeps an eye on the ageing owners of the house, and she does the garden for them.'

'How long has she been here?'

'A few years. Come on in and meet her.'

The door was not locked, and Kate walked into a tiny hallway, with Miranda following close behind her.

'Mum!' Kate called.

A door opened to the left, and a woman appeared whose smiling face made it abundantly clear how delighted she was to see them both. Miranda noticed that Kate's mother looked very fit, although she sensed that she must be some years older than she seemed. She wasn't quite as tall as her daughter, and her build was stockier. Her dark hair was speckled with grey, but was healthy and strong. She was wearing a thick jumper and well-worn jeans.

'Come in, come in,' she invited. 'You must be Miranda. I'm Sylvia. I'm so glad you could come. I've got a big pan of thick soup simmering in the kitchen. I didn't know how hungry you two would be, so I thought that was the best solution. Let's put your bags in the corner here, ready for tonight.'

Miranda could smell the soup, and to her embarrassment, her stomach rumbled loudly.

Sylvia chuckled. 'Come into the kitchen and take as much soup as you want.'

The kitchen was a small lean-to at the back of the cottage. Sylvia took some earthenware bowls out of a low cupboard.

'It smells wonderful,' said Miranda appreciatively.

Sylvia lifted the lid of the pan, and handed her a ladle.

'There's quite a lot in there that I grew in the garden this year – carrots, leeks, parsnips, potatoes, fennel and herbs. The vegetable patch is quite big. I'll show it to you tomorrow if you're interested. There's a wall at the bottom that catches the sun, and it gives good shelter, too.'

Miranda filled up her bowl and then handed the ladle to Kate. There was a small table with two chairs.

'Take a seat,' Sylvia said. 'I'll perch on the kitchen stool.'

Miranda settled herself, and sipped from an old-fashioned soup spoon that Sylvia had handed across to her. 'It's absolutely delicious!' she exclaimed. 'You must give me a complete list of the ingredients.'

'Certainly,' Sylvia replied.

Kate laughed. 'I have to warn you that Mum's soups are unrepeatable. They only taste right when she has made them and you can sit in her kitchen. The bowls and the spoons that don't match are all part of the experience.'

'Would you like some bread with it?' asked Sylvia.

'That would be nice,' Miranda replied.

Sylvia took some rolls out of a bread bin, and put them on a plate. 'I've plenty more.'

Miranda took a bite out of one of them. 'This tastes homemade,' she commented appreciatively.

'I prefer my own,' Sylvia told her.

Miranda ate in silence for a few minutes, and then asked, 'Sylvia, how did you find this place?'

'Actually, it's quite an interesting story. I needed some work, and I saw an advert in a magazine that said an elderly couple were looking for help with their house and garden. There was no indication that accommodation might be available. At the time I was living in a small rented flat in the centre of Tronton. The phone number that was given wasn't local. I rang it the next day, and found myself talking to a niece of the people who wanted help. We had a long talk, and then it was arranged that I would go to visit the couple – Mr and Mrs Peterson – a few days later. We liked each other straight away. They showed me round the house and garden, and when they saw how happy I was with the idea of working for them, Mr Peterson said that they might be able to offer accommodation, if I was interested. I asked what he had in mind, and he told me that they were planning to do up the gardener's cottage. I had certainly noticed this building, but it had obviously seen better days, and I had assumed that they had lost any interest in it. He explained that they had planned merely to make it weatherproof again, but if I was interested they would also make it habitable. I was overjoyed. Its situation is perfect for me. My little flat was okay, and I had good neighbours, but this place is a real haven. You won't believe it, but I've got it rent free for as long as I am working for the Petersons.'

'That's wonderful!' Miranda exclaimed.

'Kate might have told you already, but when her dad left us, I really struggled for money, and it's only since I got this place that I've felt comfortable financially.'

Miranda noticed that Kate had winced at the mention of her father, and that she immediately turned the conversation away from him by saying, 'I've not seen much of the Petersons myself, but they have always been friendly to me.'

'Yes, they live very quietly,' said Sylvia. 'Mr Peterson has a lot of hobbies like stamp collecting and repairing old clocks, and Mrs Peterson does some stunning needlework. Occasionally people come to the house to see these things, and then I'm asked to provide something to eat, but usually I only do some washing and cleaning.' She turned to Kate. 'I don't think I've told you the most recent development.'

'What's that?' asked Kate.

Miranda could see that she was trying hard to conceal a feeling of alarm, and her shoulders looked very tight and hunched.

'Tell me,' Kate pressed.

Sylvia began. 'It could be very good news.'

Kate's shoulders relaxed.

'A few weeks ago, their niece came to stay with them. She was here for almost a week. I cooked an evening meal for them all each day. Near the end of her stay, they invited me to join them in the afternoon. I was a bit anxious in case they were going to tell me of a change in circumstances that might affect me adversely. But after some general conversation, Mr Peterson put forward a plan that he wanted me to consider. He said that although they were still in good enough health, they knew that this would not go on forever. He emphasised how much they valued my help. Then he asked if we could discuss how much help I could offer in the future. I replied that I could certainly continue providing the same, and could possibly also do more if needed. He said that they wondered if I would oversee any extra help they might need in the future. This sounded like a reasonable proposition, and I agreed. I added that of course it was dependent on my own health, which they accepted. After that I could barely believe my ears. He said that if I were willing to stay for at least another seven years, they would give the cottage to me! Patricia – the niece – said that she would eventually inherit the house, and that she agreed entirely with their offer.'

Kate stared at her mother. She opened her mouth to say something, but nothing came out.

'That's amazing news,' said Miranda warmly. 'It shows just how much they value you. I'm so impressed that they have no intention of trying to get you to do any of the hard work of looking after them if they become ill.'

Sylvia went on. 'They are in the middle of drawing up the necessary papers with their solicitor, which will guarantee my ownership after I have worked for them for another seven years.'

'What happens if you get ill yourself before then?' asked Kate in a whisper.

'They have said that so long as I am able to help by overseeing their care, they will pay for a cleaner and a gardener to do the other work.'

Kate was clearly overjoyed. She jumped up and flung her arms around her mother, hugging her so tightly that she had to beg to be allowed to breathe.

'Why on earth didn't you phone me straight away?' Kate demanded.

Sylvia looked bemused. 'Actually I think I'm still in a state of shock about it. I never expected in my wildest dreams that I would be given such an incredible opportunity. And there's part of me that can't believe it until the documentation is drawn up, and I have a signed copy in my hand.'

'I can understand that,' said Miranda. 'I think I'd be exactly the same.' She turned to Kate, and to her consternation, she saw that tears were pouring down her cheeks. 'What is it?' she asked, putting her arm round her.

Kate shook her head mutely.

'No, you've got to tell us,' Miranda told her firmly.

'Let's go and sit in the other room,' Sylvia suggested. 'It's a bit warmer in there, and we can relax. I'll fetch some more logs, and give the fire a poke.'

It was then that Miranda remembered the large bag of chestnuts that she had brought with her, but she said nothing, as she was determined to find out what was troubling Kate.

She seated herself close to her, and passed her a clean tissue out of her handbag. 'What is it?' she asked again.

Sylvia bustled in, carrying two substantial logs under one arm, and attended to the fire before settling herself.

She addressed Kate. 'What is it, dear?'

Kate shook her head again, desperately trying to stem the flow of tears that were still running down her cheeks, but the tissue that Miranda had provided was now sodden. Sylvia rummaged around in a low cupboard at one side of the fireplace, and produced a rag, which she handed to her daughter.

'Here you are,' she said. 'This should do the job. It's one of the rags I tore out of an old flannelette nightie. It's nice and soft.'

Kate buried her face in it for a few minutes, before blowing her nose loudly.

'I'm afraid of saying something that'll upset you, Mum.'

'Well, one thing's certain. There's already someone who's very upset, and that's you,' replied Sylvia matter-of-factly.

'I've been so worried about you,' Kate blurted out.

'Whatever for?' asked her mother. 'As you can see, I'm fine.'

'I've worried about you ever since Dad left, and I couldn't tell you because I thought it would put even more stress on you.'

Miranda said nothing. It was clear to her that for now this was a conversation that belonged entirely to Kate and her mother.

Everything was silent except for the crackling from the grate as the logs began to burn.

Miranda reckoned that it must have been a full five minutes before Sylvia spoke.

'Kate, it strikes me that there've been things we haven't known about each other. Maybe that was best at the time, but if it was, it certainly isn't right any more.'

Miranda began to feel a bit uncomfortable. 'If you would like some time on your own together, I could go out for a walk,' she offered.

'Don't be silly, Miranda,' said Kate. 'You're my best friend, and you're a welcome guest.'

'I don't think it's silly,' Miranda objected. 'You and you mother might want privacy to do some catching up, and I can easily pop out for an hour or so.'

'Nonsense!' exclaimed Sylvia. 'I would never agree to that. Anything that Kate and I have to say to each other can be done while you're here.' She paused. 'That is, if you won't find it too stressful.'

'Maybe this is the time when we should tell your mum about our plans,' Miranda suggested.

Kate's face broke into a smile. 'That's a great idea! You start.'

'Kate's going to let her flat and come and live with me for a while.'

Sylvia opened her mouth to say something, shut it again, and then said, 'Go on.'

Kate interrupted. 'Don't worry, I'm going to pay my way.'

Sylvia relaxed.

Miranda continued. 'We've both got to find a way forward with our lives.'

'Work life and love life,' Kate added bluntly. 'We've realised that there have been things we've both been avoiding, and we're going to help each other with that.'

'That sounds a grand plan,' Sylvia approved. 'Can I ask what you've been avoiding?'

Miranda blushed. 'Some of it's rather personal.'

'I don't want to pry,' said Sylvia hurriedly. 'It's just that...'

'Sylvia, I haven't told you yet, but I've brought with me a huge bag of chestnuts,' said Miranda brightly. 'Shall I dig it out, and we can roast some of them on the fire?'

'Chestnuts? The perfect way to spend Christmas Eve is roasting chestnuts. I looked for some yesterday when I was out shopping, but they were very poor, and I didn't buy any. If you give me a handful, I'll put them in the embers at the front of the fire and keep an eye on them.'

The evening was spent snug and warm. After enjoying hot chestnuts, Miranda tentatively suggested that they might sing some carols.

Kate seized upon this idea enthusiastically. 'Silent Night first,' she announced. 'I can sing alto.'

The result was very pleasing. While Miranda and Kate sang the words, Sylvia added some low notes in harmony.

'Aren't we good?' said Kate. 'Pity I don't know the alto part for any of the others.'

Miranda smiled. 'Never mind about that. I think we should carry on however we can.'

Several carols later, they sat and talked over hot drinks.

Sylvia turned to Kate. 'I have some more news.'

'Mum, I can't believe this. Out with it. What's your next secret?'

'Graham phoned yesterday evening.'

Miranda saw Kate's buoyant mood crumble, although she struggled hard to hide this.

'The news is good,' said Sylvia quietly.

Kate clutched her mug tightly with both hands, and waited.

'He's got a job.'

'A job…' echoed Kate weakly.

'Yes, the rehab team contacted him a few weeks ago. Apparently there was a temporary job available for someone who could provide buddying for young people who were out of control with alcohol.'

'Is it wise?' Kate could not keep her worry hidden. 'I thought the voluntary job at the Oxfam Bookshop was suiting him. From what you've told me, he's developed quite an interest in the older books that come in.'

'The rehab team had been so impressed by the real changes in Graham's attitudes and insight that they felt he was the man for the job.'

'They might have got it wrong. Oh, Mum, I don't want to sound negative, but it's taken him so long to get off that stuff, and surely there's a risk that he'll be drawn back into drinking too much.'

'Kate, the job is only for six months. I feel sure he'll manage. He'll know by the end of that time whether or not he's cut out for it. And he'll be working as part of a team.'

'Six months,' Kate mused. She began to feel hopeful. 'If it

goes well, he'll have something really positive to put on his CV. And feeling valued as a team member might be the next step forward.'

Thus far Miranda had felt it best not to say anything, but now she added, 'Kate, I haven't met your brother, and I know very little about him, but this does sound like a good opportunity.'

'This is turning out to be an interesting Christmas,' Kate remarked as lightly as she could, but Miranda could see that she was on the verge of tears again. Kate continued. 'I think I could do with some shut-eye now.'

'I'll bring the bedding through,' said Sylvia, and she disappeared into the bedroom, returning soon afterwards with her arms full of pillows.

Miranda took them from her, and then said to Kate, 'I haven't been in touch with Amber and Jessica, so I'm wondering about sending a text.'

'Did you send them a card?' Kate asked, almost accusingly.

'Of course I did.'

'Then you *have* been in touch with them. Have they sent you a card or a text or something?'

Miranda felt bemused. She didn't know what her friend was getting at. 'No, that's why I might send a text now.'

Kate looked straight into her friend's eyes and said only one word, 'Plague.'

Miranda's hand flew to her mouth. 'Oh!' she exclaimed.

'Yes, "oh" indeed,' Kate said meaningfully.

Sylvia appeared with two duvets. 'Will you need anything else?'

'We'll be fine, Mum,' Kate replied. 'You have the bathroom first. Miranda and I have something to talk over while we clear up in the kitchen.'

In the kitchen, Miranda assured Kate that she needed no further prompting.

'That's good news, but I'll keep an eye on you,' Kate assured her. 'Now, there's something I've got to say before we roll out our camping mats. I haven't told Mum that my job's finished.'

Miranda was thoughtful. 'Mm... I can see why, but I'm not sure it's the right decision. If you don't tell her soon, how's she going to feel when she finds out?'

'She's had two bits of good news recently, so I don't want her to have some bad news right now,' said Kate sharply. 'I'd like to wait until I've got something else sorted out, then it won't seem like such bad news to her.'

Miranda made no further comment, and it was not long before they were settling down to sleep.

Chapter Six

The next morning, Kate and Miranda woke to find some huge old socks in the fireplace, bulging with unknown contents. Everything was completely silent.

'Mum!' Kate called, but there was no reply. She got up, went into the kitchen, and peered through the window. Then she shouted excitedly for Miranda to join her.

'Oh, wow!' Miranda exclaimed. She could see that a light fall of snow had decorated all the trees and bushes, and everything looked quite magical.

Kate shivered. 'Let's get dressed and tidy away the bed. Then we can start the fire again. I expect Mum's outside somewhere.'

They had just got the fire going, and were about to investigate the bulges in the stockings, when they heard Sylvia come in through the back door.

'Thanks, Santa,' Kate called out.

'You're up,' Sylvia observed. 'Happy Christmas! I'll join you in a minute. I'm in the middle of feeding the birds, and I'm going to take some water out for them. Everything out there is frozen solid.'

Miranda searched through her overnight bag and produced a small parcel. 'I brought this for your mum,' she told Kate. 'Let's wait until she comes back before we look in the stockings.'

'Good idea,' Kate agreed. 'I've got something for her, and for you as well.'

Miranda smiled. 'I've got you something to add to your earring collection.'

'Great! I can't wait to see.'

Sylvia popped her head round the door from the kitchen.

'Want some hot porridge?'

'I don't want to put you to any trouble,' said Miranda politely.

'It's no trouble at all. I made it before I went out. It's sitting in the pan here, all hot and ready. I'm certainly having some. It keeps me warm.'

Miranda relaxed. 'In that case, I'd love some. I'll come and get it.'

'You can stay where you are. I'll bring it.'

When they had finished eating, Miranda handed the small parcel to Sylvia. 'Merry Christmas!'

Sylvia looked embarrassed. 'You shouldn't have bothered.' Carefully she eased the sellotape from the wrapping paper. 'How lovely!' she exclaimed as she revealed a glass paperweight with a snow scene inside it. She put it on the mantelshelf and admired it again. 'The design is so intricate. Thank you so much.'

Kate and Miranda found that the socks were stuffed with pieces of fruit, with some nuts in the toe end of each.

Kate began to munch her way through a large apple. 'Mm... This is delicious,' she pronounced.

'That one was grown here,' Sylvia told her. 'There's an apple tree trained up the wall at the bottom of the garden, and its apples keep well.'

Kate handed a rectangular parcel to her mother and one to Miranda. Sylvia unwrapped hers to find a book about unusual beans. She was soon engrossed in it.

'It gives information about the origin of each variety, and in the back is a list of suppliers,' she said excitedly.

Miranda's book was about Spanish dancing, and she was very pleased with it. 'I'll enjoy reading this. Thanks, Kate.'

'And now...' Kate announced with an air of drama, 'I'm going to open this!' She ripped the paper off the present that Miranda handed to her, revealing a small box. Inside was a pair of earrings, and from each earring was suspended a tiny replica of a robin. 'Oh, these are wonderful!' she exclaimed. 'I must put them on immediately! Then I'll rush into the garden and join in at the seed feeders. Miranda, this is an ingenious idea.' She winked at her. 'And it'll certainly add a different flavour to my next dinner date.'

'Actually, I'd love to see round the garden,' said Miranda.

Sylvia stood up. 'I'll gladly give you a guided tour. You'll be fine with your shoes, because any mud's well frozen.'

Miranda wandered after Sylvia down the path that ran alongside a substantial border by the extensive lawn.

'The herbaceous border is glorious in the summer,' Sylvia told her. 'There were some surprisingly interesting plants in it when I came, although it was quite a task rescuing them from among the weeds. The Petersons and I have added to them since.'

Miranda was astonished by the size of the vegetable garden.

'I didn't tell you because I wanted you to get a surprise,' Kate said. 'You should see it in the summer. Under Mum's ministrations it's stunning.'

Sylvia smiled. 'You must come back and see it.'

Just then, Miranda noticed a spider's web that was spread between the strong stalks of some dead vegetation. She pointed to it. Snow had accentuated the visual impact, making the intricate latticework stand out.

'It's almost glowing.' Miranda whispered, as if she feared that the sound of her voice would disturb it.

A moment later, a robin landed at Kate's feet, and she was almost mesmerised. 'Perhaps it spotted my earrings,' she murmured.

Sylvia chuckled. 'No, that's my little companion when I'm out here working.'

Back in the cottage, Sylvia pointed to the phone and said, 'Miranda, if there's anyone you want to ring while you're here, just go ahead.'

'I've got my mobile with me, thanks. I'll phone my parents later.'

'You might find it hasn't got much signal here. Why not

phone them now, while Kate and I mix up the stuffing for the turkey breast?'

Although this offer was clearly genuine, Miranda sensed that Sylvia wanted to say something to Kate in private, so she decided to take up her suggestion. She had a relaxed conversation with her parents, telling them about the Petersons, Sylvia, the cottage and the garden. After that, she picked up the book that Kate had given her, and began to study it.

In the kitchen, Sylvia and Kate were deep in conversation. They had begun a little slowly, but things had soon flowed, and later they moved into difficult territory.

'Mum, is there anything else I should know?' asked Kate.

Sylvia cleared her throat. 'Your dad tried to get in touch,' she said bluntly.

'Oh no!' exclaimed Kate angrily.

Sylvia touched her daughter's arm. 'He sent a letter to the flat, and someone forwarded it here. I burned it.'

Kate felt a whirlwind of emotions inside her. She was furious that her father had showed that he still existed, but at the same time she had felt a fleeting surge of hope that he was going to do something useful for once. Her mother had burned the letter, so she would never know. She bit her lip.

'Kate, the only thing I ever wanted out of him was to help Graham, but Graham's helping himself now, and in any case I can't imagine that your dad would do anything but upset him.'

'What about me?' The words were out of Kate's mouth before she could stop them.

Sylvia froze for a moment, before passing a pot of dried herbs to Kate. 'Sprinkle some of these into the mixture,' she instructed. There was silence, and then she asked quietly, 'What is it you want from him?'

Kate decided to be as honest as she could. 'I need to get out of the mess I'm in, and what he did has played a big part in creating it.'

Sylvia looked at her daughter with a penetrating stare. 'What exactly do you mean?'

Kate felt very uncomfortable. She had said things that she had not planned to say. In fact, she had barely even known them until she heard herself speak. She stirred the mixture slowly and deliberately. Then she said, 'Mum, I don't want to talk about this today. It's Christmas, and I want us all to enjoy ourselves.'

Sylvia was reluctant to let the subject go. 'It's the first time you've said anything about this, and it sounds serious. Do you really think I can enjoy myself if I know that you're struggling?'

'I'll tell you something about it tomorrow,' Kate promised. She touched her mother's arm. 'I won't find it easy, but I'll try.'

Sylvia smiled. 'Let's get on with stuffing the turkey breast. I want to have it in the oven soon. The best result comes from cooking it for a long time at a moderate heat.'

'I'd like us to make up some sandwiches, and take Miranda for a walk to see some of the countryside around here.'

'Sounds good to me.'

The air was fresh and crisp. They all walked until dusk, and then returned to the cottage, where they added potatoes to the contents of the oven. After that they cleaned out the grate again and soon had a good fire burning. Conversation flowed freely. Sylvia made them laugh by telling some funny stories that had been handed down in her family, and then she surprised them by suggesting that they all made something together that would be a reminder of their visit.

'Any ideas?' asked Kate.

'I'm up for it,' Miranda agreed, 'but I can't think of anything at the moment.'

'I'll pop into the kitchen for a few minutes,' said Sylvia, and you two can work something out.'

'Don't you want a hand?' Miranda asked.

Sylvia shook her head, and left them to consider.

'I've an idea!' said Miranda suddenly.

'That's good news, because my mind's a blank.'

'We could make a collage.'

'Perfect! Let's go into the garden and collect some

62

materials.'

In the kitchen, Kate took a bag, a pair of strong scissors and the large torch that was kept near the door.

'Where are you off to?' asked her mother.

'Don't worry, we'll be back soon,' Kate assured her. 'Miranda's got a plan.'

The rest of the evening was spent eating, and then creating the collage.

As they worked on it together, Sylvia was clearly excited. 'I can put it up on the wall, and I can add bits to it later. In fact...' She stood up and disappeared into her room for a few minutes, returning carrying a cardboard box. 'I've got some interesting scraps of material we can use.'

Their project kept them up late, and it was after midnight by the time they all went to bed.

Chapter Seven

Kate woke first the following morning, and she waited patiently for Miranda to open her eyes.

'What time is it?' asked Miranda sleepily.

'About nine. I've been waiting for you to stir. Miranda, when I was in the kitchen with Mum yesterday, I blew it.'

Miranda was now fully alert. 'Blew what?'

Kate told her exactly what had taken place.

'So we're going to talk to your mum about our jobs after all.'

'And probably men, too.'

'I don't think I want to do that.'

'I meant just me.'

'When?'

'Not sure yet. Depends on what we're doing for the rest of the day.'

Over breakfast, Sylvia informed them that the Petersons had asked them round for a cup of tea in the afternoon.

'That's kind of them,' Miranda commented.

'Why didn't you tell us before?' asked Kate.

'No particular reason,' said Sylvia evasively.

Kate did not press her mother, and instead asked bluntly, 'When shall we have our talk?'

'I think we should start now,' said Sylvia quietly.

'Mum, I wasn't going to tell you yet, but I've been made redundant.'

Shock registered on Sylvia's face.

'So have I,' Miranda added. 'In fact, I've been out of work for about two months now.'

Kate snorted. 'Yes, they waited a bit longer before they got rid of me. And there were quite a few of us finished this month.'

'What are you going to do?' Sylvia's face was etched with worry.

'You know the first step already. I'm letting my flat out and moving in with Miranda. One plan might be to get temporary jobs in something completely different.'

'Neither of us is sure yet,' Miranda explained. 'I've been thinking about retraining, but I don't feel drawn to anything in particular.'

Kate's voice was tight. 'When I was young, I wanted to be a teacher like Dad, but that all went down the pan after he went off and did what he did. After that, I didn't want to be like him any more.'

Sylvia noticed at this point that Kate sounded more like a teenager than an adult woman, but she made no comment.

'Well, you're both energetic and able young women,' she said sincerely. 'I'm sure you'll make something good come out of this.'

Kate's face broke into a smile. 'Thanks for that vote of confidence. It's just what I needed. It's all a bit scary, but I was in the wrong kind of job anyway.'

'Me, too,' added Miranda. 'You see, Sylvia, I've been too much of a mother to my two younger sisters, and I've not been concentrating enough on myself and my own future.'

Sylvia nodded. 'I've come across that kind of thing before.'

Miranda went on. 'I've only realised it recently, with the help of Kate and another friend.'

'Good friends are invaluable,' Sylvia mused. 'Things can fall into place with the right kind of conversation.'

Miranda could see that Sylvia was talking about her own experience as much as that of herself and Kate. She would have liked to ask what was in Sylvia's mind at that moment, but she didn't feel she knew her well enough yet. Instead she said, 'I got quite low at first when I lost my job.'

'She hid and stopped eating,' added Kate.

'Not exactly,' Miranda corrected her. 'I did lose quite a bit of weight, and I sort of forgot to keep in touch with people for a while.'

Sylvia was sympathetic. 'It's all too easy for that to happen when you've had a shock. I was a bit like that when Kate's dad left me, but I had to keep going because of Graham and Kate.'

'Mum, is there anything you need a hand with while we're here?' Kate asked.

'I haven't got anything in mind, but I'll think about it.'

'Miranda and I will have to catch a train about lunchtime tomorrow,' Kate warned.

Her mother smiled. 'I remember, but I don't think there's anything I need before then, except...'

'We'd like to help,' Miranda assured her. 'What's in your mind?'

'I was planning to take a look in the loft some time soon,' Sylvia replied. 'It might be best to do that while someone's around.'

Kate's eyes flashed. 'Mum!' she said reprovingly. 'You don't mean that you would have done that on your own?'

Sylvia seemed not to notice Kate's indignation. 'When I first moved in, I stood on the top of a ladder and had a look in,' she mused. 'It's actually quite spacious.'

'My loft's pretty good,' Miranda told her. 'It's going to come in handy for storage while Kate and I are living together.'

'It's not just storage I'm thinking of,' Sylvia explained. 'Oh, I know it's a long way off, but when this place is mine, perhaps I could put a spare room up there.'

'We could have a good look, but my guess is there'd be a problem with access,' said Kate. 'It would probably be better to build something out at the back.'

'At the moment I've no idea how much ground I'll get, and what restrictions might be placed on the use of it,' Sylvia pointed out. 'Now,' she added briskly, 'I shouldn't bother with all this daydreaming. Seven years from now is a long time away. I'll have a quick look in the loft while you're here, and leave it at that.'

But Kate and Miranda persisted.

'I don't see why you shouldn't think of a plan, and start saving up,' Kate asserted.

'Kate told me you like having people to stay, and a spare room would be really useful,' Miranda added.

'That's true,' Sylvia acknowledged. 'And I heard of something recently that I really liked the sound of.'

'Go on,' Kate encouraged.

'There's an organisation called Women Welcome Women. If you need a room to stay for a day or so, you can look on the website and see who's offering one nearby. I can't go travelling about myself, but I would love to have people to stay here. Who knows, I might meet new people from all over the world.'

Miranda could see that Sylvia's face almost glowed as she thought about this.

'Where's the ladder, Mum?' asked Kate. 'Let's get on with the reconnaissance.'

'It's in the shed by the vegetable garden.'

'Miranda and I will get it,' Kate announced decisively.

'The shed's padlocked. The key is hanging in the kitchen, just above the worktop.'

Once out of Sylvia's hearing, Miranda said excitedly, 'Isn't that a great idea of your mum's?'

'Fabulous! And how I wish I was in a position to help her to get her dream.'

'Stage one is to help her look in the loft,' Miranda reminded her. 'And remember, we've got to fix ourselves before we can fix anyone else.'

'That doesn't stop me wishing, though,' Kate replied.

'You're allowed to wish, but after that you've got to put your energy into thinking about yourself.'

'Oh, I know… Plague, plague, plague…' said Kate crossly. 'Miranda, it's so tempting…'

'I think I know what you mean. If you put lots of energy into helping other people, it can make you feel good…'

'... but that can mean you forget about helping yourself!' Kate finished for her.

Miranda went on. 'All you have to do is to think of my situation. Look at all the energy I've put into helping Amber and Jessica to grow up, when I should have been using more of it for me and my future.'

'Precisely,' Kate agreed with alacrity. 'It's more than all right to help, but if helping someone else is instead of helping yourself, then it's wrong.'

By this time they were back at the cottage with the ladder, and steered it carefully through the kitchen.

'Come this way! The access hatch is in my room,' Sylvia called.

It was not long before Sylvia was at the top of the ladder, torch in hand. 'Can you hold the ladder steady?' she asked. 'I'd like to climb in.'

'Be careful,' Kate warned.

Miranda was impressed by the ease with which Sylvia swung herself into the loft. She disappeared from view, but Miranda and Kate could see the beam of the torch flashing to and fro as she examined the space.

'What's it like?' shouted Kate.

'Much better than I had remembered,' Sylvia called back. 'Could you pass the measuring tape from the mantelshelf, and a pencil and paper. I'll make a few notes while I'm up here.'

Kate fetched these and passed them up. It was not long before Sylvia reappeared at the hatch.

'I'm finished,' she announced.

Kate began to giggle.

'What's so funny?' asked her mother crossly.

'You've got a huge spider dangling off your hair,' Kate told her.

To Miranda's surprise, Sylvia gently explored round her head until she located the thread from which the spider was suspended. She had fully expected Sylvia to be alarmed.

'I'll make sure I leave him here, safe and sound,' Sylvia

68

said lovingly. Once back in the room again, she added, 'Thanks very much. I'll be able to think about these measurements when I'm dreaming in front of the fire.'

The visit to the Petersons' was very enjoyable. The time rushed past, and in the end they stayed far longer than was originally intended.

As they sat in front of the log fire that evening, Miranda brought out the rest of the chestnuts, and they shared them as they talked.

'I wish you were here longer,' Sylvia admitted. 'I'll miss you both. Don't hesitate to give me a ring any time you want to come back again.'

'That's very kind,' said Miranda.

'And I hope that by the next time you come your future will be more secure,' Sylvia added.

'Well, we're going to do our best,' Kate replied. 'It's been great being here, Mum. I feel I've got some of my energy back.'

Chapter Eight

As they boarded the train back to Branton, Miranda and Kate found that there were plenty of spare seats, so they were able to sit together for the whole journey.

'I'm so glad I came with you to see your mum,' said Miranda.

'So am I,' replied Kate. 'If she and I had been on our own, it would have been okay, but I got a lot more out of it with you there, and I'm sure Mum did, too.'

'I've made some important decisions,' Miranda announced quietly.

Kate sat bolt upright. 'Decisions? Why didn't you say something straight away?'

'I wanted time to mull things over, and the last few days have been perfect for that.'

'But tell me what you've decided,' Kate insisted impatiently.

'I'm going to start by doing some modules at college.'

'That's not exactly high flying.' Kate was surprised to hear Miranda's decision, as she had imagined she might have chosen something more challenging.

'I know that,' Miranda replied abruptly. If she were honest, she felt a little hurt by Kate's response, but did not want to say so.

But Kate had realised her mistake. 'Sorry. Tell me the rest. I'm intrigued.'

'I might go on to do some more intensive study, but this way I hope to build up some confidence first.'

'You're very bright,' Kate assured her. 'Surely you could go straight into some vocational training or something.'

'Well, there's another reason for the modules,' Miranda

explained. 'I want to do some accounting and marketing, and things like that, because I'm thinking of starting up in business.'

'You never cease to amaze me!' exclaimed Kate. 'What business do you have in mind?'

'That's something I'm not sure about.'

'But you must have some ideas.'

Miranda was evasive. 'Well, er...'

'Come on. Out with it!'

'These conversations I've been having with Tess about her wedding...' Here Miranda's voice trailed off.

'You mean they've put you off the idea of ever getting married, and you're thinking about a career in business instead?'

'No, not at all. In fact, I've found myself becoming more and more interested in all the details she tells me. It's fascinating.'

Kate was stunned. 'If someone had told me that I'd be sitting on a train with you while you spoke about how fascinating wedding chat is, I wouldn't have believed them. I would have thought they were off their trolley. Miranda, what's going on?'

'It's a surprise to me, too. I keep imagining wedding gowns in various designs, outfits for central guests, a choice of interesting venues, a range of buffets, innovative wedding gifts...' She sighed. 'The list goes on and on.'

'Well, continue,' Kate encouraged.

'My dream is to run a business where a couple can come and discuss their wedding plans. I will have developed links to many fascinating and unusual resources that I can put in front of my clients, so that when everything has been agreed, I go ahead and bring it all together for the big day. The service I want to offer will be very personal. The care I will provide will be something that the couple will remember for years to come, and the diversity of options will include things that people have never thought of. Kate, when I get back home I'm going to sit and sketch some of the clothes designs that have been coming into my mind. I can't wait!' She rushed on. 'I want to source a range of fabulous materials for the gowns, and I need to make contact with good dressmakers.'

Kate began to feel a little nervous. She had never heard Miranda speak like this before. For a moment she wondered if the stress of unemployment and weight loss had somehow affected her friend more than she might have predicted. But Miranda had said she had savings to tide her over, her parents were going to help with the costs of further study, and she had already put on a lot of the weight she had lost, so she couldn't be feeling too bad. No, there must be some other explanation for this sudden change.

Miranda's voice broke into her thoughts. 'You're very quiet. What's the matter?'

Kate hesitated for a moment, and then made up her mind to be forthright. 'I was worrying about you, but I'd managed to work out that I don't need to.'

'That's certainly the right conclusion,' Miranda assured her. 'If I can make my business plans work, I'll definitely look back on my redundancy as a blessing in disguise. That job was awful! And it's not just being away from the horrible job that's helping me. You and June have been pointing out things about the way I relate to my sisters. That's been so helpful. I knew there was something wrong, but I thought it would be fine if only they got in touch a bit more. Now I know differently. And the other thing is that you and I are going to be living together for a while. That's going to be really good for both of us.' She paused for a moment, and then added emphatically, 'I'm certain.'

Kate grinned. 'Yes, we need to keep an eye on each other's love life... or lack of it, to be precise.' She giggled. 'It feels like a cliff face, but on the other hand it could be fun.'

Miranda smiled at her friend. 'I sincerely hope so. Kate, when will you be able to move in?'

'I got the impression when I spoke to the agent that he had someone in mind already.'

'You should phone him as soon as you get back,' Miranda

advised.

'I promise. Pity I don't have his number with me.' Kate fell silent for a few minutes. Then she said, 'I get paid until the end of the year. Miranda, I've been thinking seriously about the dog-walking option. Even if I had enough spare money, I need to be getting on with something. Dog walking would give me a small income, plenty of exercise and enough time to think. Added to that, I would enjoy it. The only problem is how to get started.'

'I'll help you to make up some cards to put in local shops,' Miranda offered. 'And I could ask around, too. I might even manage to talk to Malcolm about it. He's meeting a lot of people all the time.'

Kate interrupted. 'Plague!'

For a moment Miranda was puzzled, and then she began to realise what Kate meant.

Kate continued. 'You shouldn't be putting too much energy into planning how to help me. I appreciate your thoughts, but you need to get on with planning your own work. There's going to be a lot involved in that, and you mustn't get distracted.'

'That shouldn't mean I can't help at all,' Miranda objected.

'I'm not saying that. I want to help you with your business, too. It's getting the right balance that's important.'

'I expect there won't be anyone at the college over the holidays, but I'll soon be able to get my name on to some of the short courses I've seen for this term. Meanwhile, I can begin my research.'

Kate was enthusiastic. 'Great! That means we've both decided the first steps to take.'

'Kate,' said Miranda in confiding tones. 'I've an idea where some of my inspiration might be coming from. I think it's to do with my granny – Granny Ann.'

'Which granny was that?'

'She was my mum's mother.'

'Tell me about her.'

'She was wonderful,' Miranda began. Then she went on to

tell Kate the things she remembered most about her, including the secret admirer.

'Ah!' said Kate. 'So she was nearly forty when she got married. That means there's hope for us after all.'

Miranda kicked her friend gently. 'The important thing for me at the moment is everything she told me about her life before then.'

For a moment Kate behaved as if Miranda had not spoken. 'A secret admirer? I wish we knew more about him. No, actually, I could do with one myself,' she joked. Then she went on to say, 'I always knew you had an eye for colour and style, and it puzzled me that you didn't use it much for your own benefit. Miranda, how old were you when Granny Ann died?'

'Five, I think.' Miranda felt miserable as she recalled the feeling of emptiness that followed. 'It wasn't long before Amber was born, and Jessica soon after.'

'Aha! So instead of having your lovely granny, you helped to look after babies,' Kate pointed out perceptively.

'When you put it like that, I can't avoid agreeing.'

'And now you're not looking after them, you're remembering all the colour and excitement that Granny Ann filled your head with.'

Miranda gaped. 'You're right!' she exclaimed. 'You're absolutely right!'

Kate studied her fingernails with a casual air. 'That's what friends are for.'

Miranda glanced at her watch. 'We'll be due back in Branton soon. Better get our things together. Kate, don't forget to phone the agent as soon as you get in.'

'I've already promised. In any case, I'm keen to get on with moving in with you.'

When Miranda arrived home, she threw off her coat, and straight away began the task of packing up possessions to consign to the loft for the following months. She reassembled some cardboard boxes that she had flattened and stored in the cupboard upstairs, and soon became so engrossed in what she was doing that when there was a sound from her mobile phone she jumped. At first she felt tempted to ignore it, but then changed her mind. When she checked the messages, she found one from Kate, confirming that she had been in touch with the agent, and saying that she would phone for a chat later on.

'I'll do a bit more before having something to eat,' she said aloud. 'After that I'll give Mum a quick ring.'

She took a portion of home-made stew out of the freezer to thaw, and then, humming a cheerful tune, she carried on with the packing. This process progressed with ease, as it was very clear to her that although these possessions could be useful, by far the most important thing was for her and Kate to spend these months comfortably together.

She had nearly finished eating the stew when the phone rang.

'Oh, Mum, it's you!' she exclaimed. 'I was about to ring you.'

'A happy coincidence,' her mother remarked, laughing. 'How are you?'

'I feel great. I'm getting ready for Kate to move in, and I've already got some plans for the future.' She went on to outline what was in her mind.

'Hearing you talk like this reminds me of how my own mum could be.'

'I'm very glad to hear you say that,' Miranda told her, 'because I've got a strong feeling that I'm getting a lot of inspiration from the time I knew her.'

'But you were still quite small when she died.'

'That doesn't mean I didn't absorb things.'

'Yes, of course,' said her mother quickly.

Miranda noticed that her mother's voice had sounded a bit tight, and she asked, 'Are you feeling okay?'

'Miranda, this conversation is bringing back a lot of memories of my mother. She was a most amazing woman. I do wish she had lived longer.'

'So do I,' said Miranda. 'From the bottom of my heart.' There was a brief silence, and then she added, 'Mum, I've only got one photo of her, and it's not a terribly good one.'

'I've got plenty here that I can copy for you,' her mother replied.

Miranda felt warmed by this. 'I'll look forward to seeing them, but don't feel you have to rush.' There was another short silence, after which Miranda asked, 'How's Dad?'

'He's fine. He's not in at the moment, or I'd get him to speak to you.'

'Give him my love.' Miranda hesitated, struggled a little, and then added, 'Any news of Amber and Jessica?'

Her mother laughed. 'Not much. I believe they're partying the days away. But they'll have to come back to earth when term begins. There's a lot of hard work ahead of them. Have they been in touch with you?'

'I… Er…' said Miranda, evasively. Then she decided to say more. 'To tell you the truth, I'm a bit hurt. They often don't reply to messages I leave for them, and I've decided to back off a bit and concentrate on myself for a while.'

'I'm very glad to hear that. You were a big help to me when they were young, but it's meant that they've rather taken you for granted. If they ever complain to me about lack of contact from you, I'll tell them that they've brought it on themselves, and that they should look at their own behaviour.'

This recognition and support from her mother gave Miranda's growing confidence a further boost. And it wouldn't be all that long before she had more pictures of Granny Ann. Knowing her mother as she did, she knew that she would send them soon.

Her mother continued. 'And there's another thing. Your cousins in Australia haven't been in touch. I had a card from Gary. There was very little in it, but that's not surprising, with the death being only months ago.' She sounded very annoyed. 'Poor Gary, he doesn't deserve that kind of treatment from his own sons.'

Miranda had known that Uncle Gary's second wife, Freya, had died very suddenly due to a heart problem, and that he was inconsolable. Apparently his sons had never really taken to her, so they didn't involve themselves, but kept in close contact with their mother, Janet. Miranda had very little memory of Aunt Janet. She and Uncle Gary had emigrated around the time Jessica was born, and the marriage had broken down soon afterwards.

'What do you think Uncle Gary will do now?' asked Miranda.

'I've no idea. Of course, I suggested that he came to stay with us for a couple of months. He wasn't against the idea, but for now he seems to have lost the will to plan anything.'

Gary, her mother's older brother, had married before Miranda's parents had got together, and his sons had been born soon afterwards. Consequently, they were a few years older than Miranda. Again she remembered the feeling of being glad they were boys, so that she and Granny Ann had plenty of time together.

'Anyway,' said her mother, 'enough of all that. Let's get back to talking about your plans. Those college courses sound interesting, but don't set your sights too low. After all, you're a very intelligent young woman.'

Again a warm glow spread through Miranda. It was a real boost to hear her mother talking like this. She knew that her mother believed in her, but she hadn't been so specific before.

'I want to feel my way into this,' Miranda explained. 'The courses will give me some theory, and at the same time I'll be researching the practical. And who knows who I'll meet at college. Maybe there will be people with similar ideas.'

'Have you thought about approaching the local Business Gateway?'

'It did cross my mind, but I want to get some things together first. That way I'll have more to discuss when I ask to see an advisor.'

'I think they sometimes run useful short courses.'

'I didn't know that. Maybe I'll make contact soon after all.'

It was quite late by the time Kate phoned. Miranda was dozing in a chair, and at first wondered where the ringing noise was coming from. Then she grabbed the phone, and was glad to hear her voice.

'Sorry I'm so late,' Kate apologised. 'I hope I haven't woken you up.'

Miranda laughed. 'You have, but it was the right thing to do. After I got in, I packed away a lot of stuff to put in the loft, and then Mum and I had a chat. What's your news?'

'I hope you didn't try to get anything into the loft before I'm there to give you a hand.'

'Don't worry. I'd worked that one out.'

'Thank goodness for that. We don't want any strained muscles or broken bones.'

'But tell me what's been happening with you,' Miranda pressed.

'I was right about Nigel...'

'Nigel?'

'Yes, Nigel, the letting agent.'

Miranda was intrigued by the use of the name, but made no comment.

Kate explained. 'He certainly had someone who was looking for a flat like mine.' She went on excitedly. 'It's his sister! She needs somewhere for a few months while her house is being finished.'

'That sounds perfect!'

'I can't think of anything better,' Kate agreed. 'I'll be getting the going rate, and in addition he thinks she'll be willing to let me leave some stuff locked up in the big storage cupboard. I've to speak to her on the phone tomorrow to arrange a time for her to come and see the flat, and Nigel's getting all the papers ready for us to sign. He's pretty sure she'll want to move in as soon as possible. I'll pop in to see Salma and Kareen to put them in the picture.'

'It sounds as if destiny is smiling on us, or something,' said Miranda.

'There's more!' Kate announced dramatically.

'More?' Miranda echoed.

'It looks as if I might have some work already. I went to the agency on my way home, and there was only Nigel there, holding the fort. No other customers came, so we had a bit of a chat. I told him about the redundancies and my plans for an income meantime, and guess what...?'

'What?'

'He's a real dog lover.'

'So he might know of people who need someone to do dog-walking duties.'

'He does, but it's even better than that. He's got friends who run kennels. He's sure they'd be happy to pass on my details to anyone who's looking for the kind of services I can offer.'

'You'll be telling me next that you've got a date with Nigel,' Miranda joked.

'Well, I have... Well, sort of...' Here Kate's voice trailed off.

'Kate, you've got to tell me *everything*.'

'First I need time to catch my breath. Everything's moving so fast. My head's in a whirl.'

Miranda chuckled. 'Mine's in a whirl just listening. But don't let that stop you.'

'As he and I were talking, I could see that he was interested in me. Then I noticed quite clearly how I was trying to avoid anything that could make it lead to something else. I told him I needed to pop down the road for a minute, but would be back to go through any more details about the let. I wandered down the street, wondering what to do.'

'Do you like him?' asked Miranda matter-of-factly.

'Of course. But that's hardly the point.' Kate sounded irritated.

'Sorry. What did you decide to do?'

'I decided that at the very least I could practise being a bit more friendly. After all,' Kate added defensively, 'it fits our plans.'

'You're so right. Well done! What have you fixed up?'

'He told me that he and his neighbours share a dog. Its name is Bruno, and it's a golden retriever. So I'm going to meet Bruno soon, and we'll go for a walk together.'

Miranda was puzzled. 'I haven't heard of sharing a dog before. How does it work?'

'His neighbours, Mary and Adrian, are a couple who work mostly from home. The dog lives there during the daytime, and then goes to Nigel's most evenings, and overnight. Apart from that they sort out weekends and holidays as they go along. It sounds a very good arrangement.'

'That's very interesting.'

'Miranda, I'm determined to tackle some of the problems that come up when I try to get close to someone. Will you help?'

'*Of course* I will. We promised to help each other with exactly this, and I'm not about to back out of it.'

'Whew! It's hard being the first one to try something.'

Miranda quickly reassured her friend. 'I expect I'd feel the same if it were me. Kate, I know this is changing the subject, but I wanted to tell you that the conversation I had with Mum was more than an ordinary chat.'

'I'm happy to leave the subject of men for now,' Kate replied. 'I'm exhausted with it already.'

Miranda giggled. 'With the problems each of us have had, I'm sure there's a lot more of that to come.' She then went on to tell her friend the content of the phone call with her mother.

When she had finished, Kate let out a long breath. 'I see what you mean. There was certainly a lot in that,' she agreed.

'Somehow I felt freer afterwards, although I can't quite put it into words. Kate, do you think the time we had at your mother's has helped you? I realise that it helped me. I can't put my finger on exactly why, though.'

'Knowing that Graham's situation is changing took a huge load off me,' Kate replied. 'And the news about the cottage has, too. But even more important was a conversation I had with Mum in the kitchen when we were stuffing the turkey breast. It was about Dad. It started off with me reacting a bit like a child, but somehow it quickly turned into an adult exchange, and I felt a lot better after it. The word "freer" is a good one.'

'I know what you mean. I've been like a child in that I've never talked to Mum before about how some of my relationship with Amber and Jessica wasn't right. I've stayed as a child who needed someone else to notice. When Mum spoke about it, I was then able to say something in an adult way.'

'It's almost like breaking a spell,' Kate mused.

'That's a very good way of putting it.'

It was then that Kate noticed the time. 'It's terribly late. We've both got a lot to see to, and I think we'd better go to bed.'

'Let's speak again tomorrow evening,' Miranda suggested.

Kate was thoughtful. 'It'll depend a bit on the arrangements about Nigel's sister, and all of that, so it might be late before I can phone.'

Miranda laughed. 'I'll be waiting excitedly for your news, but if you're going to be booked up all evening, send me a text, and I'll have to wait until the next day.'

'Don't start behaving like a good mother with me!' Kate warned. 'I'll expect to hear any news about college, business plans, and whether or not you've been in touch with Malcolm.'

'Malcolm?'

'I'm teasing. Seriously, though, it'll be easier for me to do my practising with Nigel once I know that you're practising, too.'

'Okay, but I don't want to have a chat with Malcolm just so that you can feel better.'

Kate chuckled. 'I wouldn't want that either.'

Chapter Nine

Miranda tried to contact the college the following day, but found that it was shut until after New Year. She didn't want to go ahead with on-line applications, because there were some questions she wanted to ask first. She spent much of the rest of the day searching the internet for suppliers of high-quality dress materials, and sending off some e-mails requesting samples.

'I'll have to think of a business name some time soon,' she reflected as she went out for a stroll.

The weak afternoon sun was pleasant, although at the same time there was a harsh breeze, and parts of the pavements were icy. Miranda walked with her head down, bracing herself against the wind, and watching carefully where she placed her feet.

'Hi!' said a familiar voice from behind her.

She jumped, and turned. 'You startled me.'

Malcolm came abreast of her, and then walked alongside her. She could see that his boots were extremely muddy.

As if reading her thoughts he remarked, 'This frost hasn't been enough to freeze the really soggy bits of ground.'

'How's business?' she asked hurriedly.

'Not too bad, thanks. Plenty of sprouts, leeks, potatoes, carrots, parsnips... I won't bore you. I can go on forever talking about it, because it's my passion. It's on my mind all the time.'

'It has to be,' said Miranda generously, 'otherwise I expect you'd find it hard to make a living.' Inside her head there was a voice that was saying something completely different – *Oh no! I can't cope with this. I just want to think about my own business.*

Again Malcolm seemed to read her thoughts. 'That's

enough about me. What are you up to yourself these days?'

Miranda tried her best to make her voice sound casual. 'Just planning the next stages.' She had no wish to air her plans with Malcolm. All she wanted at this moment was for him to go away.

'Well, good luck to you,' he replied. 'If you don't mind, I'd better get on now.'

'Not at all,' Miranda told him. Her voice carried an entirely genuine message as a feeling of relief flooded through her.

At this, he walked off quickly, and Miranda had a strange feeling that he was somehow like a fairy story character – a giant wearing seven-league boots – as he disappeared from view. She hoped fervently that he would remain preoccupied with thoughts of parsnips, and take nothing but a passing interest in her and her life. She felt annoyed that her equanimity had been so easily disturbed. She knew that she must report this encounter to Kate, but felt very tempted to keep it from her. Maybe Kate had found it hard to tell her about Nigel. She made a mental note to ask her, and her jangled feelings slowly faded.

Miranda's evening was spent quietly. There was plenty to think about, and she was glad of the time to reflect. Her memories of Granny Ann were never very far away, and she let herself relax into the remembered magic of the times they had spent together. It was already ten thirty when she eventually checked the time, and she marvelled at how the evening had sped past.

'No sound from Kate yet,' she murmured. She found her bag and took out her mobile. 'No text.' Miranda was puzzled. She would have expected to hear from Kate by now, one way or the other. 'Never mind,' she said aloud, 'I expect she's got tied up with something, and I'll hear about it tomorrow.'

She went to bed, leaving her mobile within easy reach. Then she read a book for a little while, but soon fell asleep.

When she woke the following morning, the first thing she did was to check her mobile for messages. She found a couple of texts, both of which were from Kate. The first said: *R u still awake?* The time was midnight. The second said: *Phone me when u r awake.* The time of that one was two o'clock, and it was now half past eight.

Miranda put on her housecoat and went to the bathroom. Then she went downstairs and switched the fire on. She filled a glass with water and took several sips, after which she picked up the phone and rang Kate.

'Thank goodness! It's you at last,' Kate greeted her. 'I think I've completely messed this up.'

'I haven't been doing all that well myself,' Miranda told her. 'I got on with ideas for my business, but then I went for a walk, and who should appear but Malcolm. I just wanted him to leave me alone.'

'Were you unpleasant to him?'

'I don't think so. I just didn't try to continue a conversation.'

'That sounds okay,' Kate assured her, 'but wait until you hear the mess I made.'

'Tell me the worst first. I don't like to be kept in suspense.'

'I nearly got in a tangle with him,' Kate confessed. 'I feel so embarrassed telling you that. I wondered about keeping it from you, and then decided that would be silly.'

Miranda began to laugh, and once she had started, she could not stop.

'Don't laugh at me,' Kate pleaded. 'I feel bad enough already, without you behaving as if I'm a complete fool.'

'I'm not laughing at you,' Miranda spluttered. 'I'm remembering how yesterday I nearly made the decision not to tell you that I had bumped into Malcolm.'

At this, Kate started laughing, too.

Every time one began to calm down, the other would laugh even more, and this would provoke another burst of laughter from the first.

'My face is hurting,' Miranda gasped.

'And my sides are aching,' said Kate.

When at last they were quieter, Miranda asked, 'On a completely practical front, is Nigel's sister still interested in your flat?'

'There's no doubt at all about that. She's coming this afternoon, and she wants to move in next week... If that's all right by you, of course.'

'Take whatever date suits her. And now, tell me what happened with Nigel.'

'To cut a longish story short, I met his neighbours and I met the dog. After that, he suggested a carryout and a DVD. It all seemed pretty innocuous stuff.'

'I've got the picture. What happened next?'

'Well, he sort of... pounced on me... right when I least expected it.'

'What did you do?'

'I yelped, grabbed my coat, and rushed off into the night.'

'Oh...'

'Miranda, I've done it again... He's actually a really nice guy.'

'What exactly did he do when he pounced?'

'It's all a bit hazy,' Kate admitted. 'To tell you the truth, it might have been that I *felt* as if he had pounced, but he hadn't really.'

Miranda was mystified, and said so.

'You see, I was so relaxed, and the DVD was so interesting, that I sort of lost touch with who I was with, so that when he reached over and put his arm round my shoulders...'

'You freaked out.'

'Yes, I freaked out.'

'He must have got a terrible fright if you acted as if he had assaulted you.'

'I know,' Kate acknowledged miserably. 'And now I haven't a clue what to do.'

'Send him a text,' said Miranda firmly. 'Make it light – something like "Thanks for the nice evening. Sorry for the speedy exit." Send it right now.'

'Hang on while I do that.' Kate was so grateful for Miranda's sensible guidance. The text was soon sent.

Miranda was aware that Kate's voice sounded very subdued. She could imagine something of how she must be feeling. She had felt bad enough about how she had behaved with Malcolm, but this was something else...

'What shall I do next?' asked Kate meekly.

'You'll have to wait and see what happens.'

'But what if I don't hear anything before his sister comes round?'

'Let her in, and behave in an ordinary way. You've got to give Nigel time. Just because you've managed to text him, it doesn't mean he'll respond straight away.'

'I know. The more I think about what I did, the more ridiculous it seems. The evening was fine...'

'... and you'd like to spend another one like it soon,' Miranda finished for her.

At this, Kate seemed to pull herself together. 'Well, if I've blown it, it isn't as if he's the only person in the universe. I'll tough out today, and if he's cool with me when his sister and I sign the papers, I'll have my answer. Now, I think we should have another word about Malcolm...'

'Oh no, not him!' Miranda exclaimed. 'I thought we'd dealt with today's encounter.'

Kate persisted. 'We have, but there's going to be another one some time soon. After all, he lives nearby.'

'But I don't like him!' Miranda objected.

Kate was interested to note a hint of aggression in her voice. 'Do you really mean that?' she pressed.

'Of course I do! And why are you going on about him?' Miranda snapped angrily. 'There's nothing between us, and there never will be. I want to get on with starting my business. I told him that, and I'm telling you!'

'Miranda,' Kate began more carefully, 'I think there's more to how you're reacting at the moment than you realise.' Then she added deliberately, 'I think there's a bit of Plague going on.'

86

Miranda was still defensive. 'I don't want to talk about this any more.'

'Maybe this evening?' Kate coaxed.

'Maybe not. There'll be a lot to catch up on after you've seen Nigel's sister and all that.'

Kate was not going to give up. 'I'm sure that can wait.'

There was a catch in Miranda's voice when she replied, 'We'll see. Kate, I'll have to ring off now.' She put the phone down. Her throat felt terribly tight. Thoughts of Granny Ann swirled round in her head, and she thought she might faint. Quickly she filled a glass of water and tried to sip from it, but found that she could not swallow. The feelings of missing her granny were strong, and at this moment were just as raw as when she first heard that she had gone to heaven and wouldn't be coming back. Then she remembered when Amber was born, and how wonderful it felt to be allowed to hold her. Cuddling Amber took away the pain of Granny Ann not being there any more.

Suddenly Miranda felt extremely tired, and she decided to go upstairs and lie down for a while. She didn't fall asleep, but gradually felt more herself again. After that she resolved to talk to Kate about what had happened. She knew it wouldn't be easy, but she was determined to find a way.

When she came downstairs again, the first thing she did was to pick up her drawing pad and sketch some dress designs. Soon she was completely absorbed in her task, and did not take a break until her stomach rumbled and she realised that she had had nothing to eat all day. She longed to continue sketching, but her physical hunger had to be attended to.

It was while she was working her way through a substantial sandwich that the phone rang. Miranda felt irritated. She did not want to answer it, but in the end she picked it up.

'Who is it?' she asked in uninviting tones.

'It's me – Tess,' came the bouncy reply.

Miranda sprang to life immediately. 'Oh, Tess, it's great to hear from you. I'm in the middle of sketching some dress designs.'

'I didn't know you were into that sort of thing,' said Tess, surprised.

Miranda chuckled. Then she began to chatter excitedly. 'Actually, neither did I until very recently. Tess, I want to start a business that will provide a wide range of wedding services. I've already sent off for samples of material that might be good for wedding outfits, and I'll make contacts with local dressmakers. I've spotted some useful courses at the local college – you know… accounting, business management… that kind of thing. My head's bulging with ideas.' Miranda rushed on. 'I'll draw up a list of interesting venues, and then go and check them out. I'll source unusual wedding presents. I'll check on firms that can supply good-quality buffet meals…' As she spoke, Miranda was scribbling furiously on the back of her drawing pad. 'Tess, I'm so glad you phoned. You'll be ideal for me to bounce my ideas off.'

Tess laughed heartily. 'Miranda, I've never heard you sound so animated before. It's always been me who's launched into some news of mine, hardly giving you time to get a word in.'

'Oh, I'm sorry. I should have asked how your preparations are coming on.'

'Fine, thanks. Miranda, I'm fascinated to hear about your plans, and yes, do feel that you can use me as a sounding board while you're thinking things through. It'll be great fun to be involved in – all the excitement, and no risk. Exactly the kind of thing that suits me.'

Miranda needed no further encouragement, and again she rushed on, scribbling another note. 'And Mum said I should contact the local Business Gateway, because they might have some useful courses.'

'I'm curious to know about how all this began,' said Tess. 'Is there some romance in the air?'

'Er… I think Kate might have someone she's interested in,' Miranda replied vaguely. 'Look, Tess, I'm sorry, but I'll have to go now.'

'That's fine. Glad I caught you. Phone me soon with an update on your plans,' Tess finished cheerfully.

Miranda put the phone down. Now she felt uncomfortable. What had happened? Most of that call had been fine. In fact, she had felt almost euphoric as she had outlined some of her plans, and yet now she felt quite flat. Maybe it was something to do with Tess' question about romance. But she dismissed the idea. Her life was already packed full of colour and promise. Romance wasn't a necessary ingredient. She returned to her sketching, and once again became immersed in it.

When Miranda heard her mobile receive a text, she checked the time and found that several hours had slipped past unnoticed. The message was from Kate to say that she was on her way, and would arrive in a few minutes. Miranda put the kettle on, and did some more sketching as she waited. Soon she heard someone outside, and went to open the door.

Kate burst in, her face glowing. 'I did it!' she announced. 'I'm so proud of myself.'

'I'll make us some hot drinks, and you must tell me everything,' Miranda replied. 'This sounds exciting.'

Sipping her mint tea, Kate gave a blow-by-blow account of what had taken place.

'Michelle, Nigel's sister, arrived bang on time. She loved the flat, said she wanted to move in on January 3rd, and said I could definitely store any bulky things in the big cupboard. Then we went over to see Nigel at his office.'

'Had you had a reply from him by then?'

Kate shook her head. 'But it was okay. He looked really pleased to see me. He had all the papers ready, and when we'd finished all that, the three of us sat and had a cup of tea together. It felt perfectly normal. Michelle asked quite a lot of questions about the general locality. I gave her my mobile number, in case she needed to contact me for anything.'

Miranda was leaning forward in her chair. 'What happened

then?'

'Nigel winked at me and said that Bruno was missing me already! Of course, I felt a bit panicky, but nothing like how I'd felt when I ran away. I told him to let Bruno know that I'd come and see him again soon, and then I left.'

Miranda clapped her hands and bounced up and down in her chair.

Kate smiled. 'Thanks for the applause. It definitely helps. And now, how have you been?'

Miranda picked up her drawing pad and handed it to her friend. 'Look inside, and then read what I've written on the back.'

Kate studied the pages and gave a low whistle. 'Wow! Miranda, you *have* been busy. And the "to do" list...' She looked through the sketches again, and chose one in particular. 'I think this one is exceptional.'

'Maybe you'll order one like that when you name the day,' Miranda teased.

Kate slapped her friend's arm playfully. 'You know that's a long way off. As they say "first catch your man!" ' Then she added ruefully, 'Or perhaps it would be more accurate to say "first face enough of your problems." '

'I might be a step further forward on that front,' Miranda confided. She was aware that her heart was beating quickly, and she felt a bit shaky, but she was determined to continue. 'You'll probably remember that I was quite ratty with you on the phone this morning.'

Kate opened her mouth to say something, but Miranda stopped her.

'Don't bother trying to make it sound not as bad as it was.'

Kate said nothing, and Miranda went on.

'After I rang off, I was in quite a state.' She then recounted what had happened.

'Sounds pretty intense,' Kate commented thoughtfully. 'Shall I say what I think?'

'Go ahead.'

'I think you should mention this to your mum next time you speak to her.'

'Actually, I was wondering about that myself.'

'I've got a question, too.'

'What's that?'

Kate looked her straight in the eye and asked, 'Did you consider not telling me about this?'

Miranda's cheeks coloured a little. 'It did cross my mind,' she admitted.

'I thought so! We'll have to keep a close eye on each other.'

'I know. I can usually see when you're in "Plague", and I expect you can see when I am.'

'But it's not so easy for the sufferer to see,' Kate concluded.

'Well, I think we've covered all the difficult bits for now,' said Miranda brightly. 'When shall we bring your stuff across?'

'I'll need a day or so to sort the rest of it out. Now I know I can use the big cupboard, I'll pack a lot of it in there. Will it be okay if I move here the day before Michelle takes over my flat?'

'That's fine. But you can come before then.'

'I'd like to see Bruno some time over New Year if I can arrange it,' Kate told her with a grin.

'So long as you don't expect me to go chasing after Malcolm.'

'I know, I know,' said Kate with mock exasperation. 'You want to get on with planning your business. Frankly, I hope that Bruno has got a lot of pals who don't have two households to live in, and who need walkies. Then I can get on with building up my interim income.' She glanced at her watch. 'I'd better dash, or I'll miss the last bus.'

'Why not stay over?'

'Tempting, but I'd better get on.' And with that, Kate grabbed her coat and disappeared into the night.

Chapter Ten

Miranda had planned to spend much of the following day with June and baby Amy. The morning was clear and frosty, and she decided to set off early and walk, instead of catching the bus. She knew the local network of footpaths well, and followed a route that was largely well away from roads. She encountered a number of people along the way, all of whom were friendly and cheerful, engaging in a greeting or something that lasted a little longer. She felt invigorated, and her mind was never far away from her plans. She looked forward to talking to June about everything.

When she neared June and Simon's house, she could see June standing at the window, watching out for her.

June welcomed her in, saying, 'It's lovely to see you again. Amy's having a sleep, so we can catch up a bit on the news while we have the chance. Miranda, you're looking really well. When I saw you last, you looked thin and peaky.'

'Things have changed quite a lot since then,' Miranda explained. 'Did you have a good Christmas?'

'Yes, thanks, it was great having Simon's relatives here. How about you?'

'I went with Kate to stay with her mum for a few days. I enjoyed it a lot, and I've got an open invitation to go back any time. She lives in a small cottage in the grounds of quite a large house. It's a lovely setting.' Miranda took a quick breath. 'June, I'm desperate to tell you about my business plans.'

'I didn't know you were heading in that direction,' said June, surprised.

Miranda laughed. 'Neither did I, but now it's started, the whole thing is gathering momentum in my mind. I think about it nearly all day, and I even dream of it at night.'

'Tell me everything about it. Do you mind if I do some of my knitting while I listen?'

'Not at all. Before I start, can I see your pattern?'

June took out her knitting bag, and handed the pattern across. On the front was an illustration of a small jumper with a daisy embroidered on it.

'It's too big for her now, but at the rate I'm going, Amy might grow past it before I've finished. Miranda, I must thank you for the lovely mobile you gave her for Christmas. She's fascinated by it.'

Miranda smiled. 'I'm glad to hear that. I was certainly drawn to it in the shop.'

After this she began to recount her plans, and June listened quietly, although her needles seemed to move more quickly as Miranda showed more and more of her excitement.

'I'm so lucky to have the backing of Mum and Dad for the fees for the courses, and I've got savings I can use for getting the business off the ground. I don't want to rush at it. I'm going to build it up slowly, feeling my way as I go.'

'That's very wise,' June agreed. 'And I can imagine that some people will want help with all of the wedding arrangements, whereas others might consult you for only one or two things.'

'That's what I'm hoping. Sometimes it might be a wedding dress, sometimes something for the mother of the bride to wear, sometimes help to find a particularly interesting venue, and sometimes innovative catering. The possibilities are endless.'

'It might be best to start off with only one or two aspects of the whole process,' June mused.

'I've thought about that. If I'm on my own, I might have to decide to specialise. I'll only have a limited amount of time, and whatever I do I want to do well.' Miranda paused for a moment, and then added, 'But first I must do some careful research, and learn about basic skills of running a business.'

'It's all so exciting!' June burst out. 'And I wish I could help.'

'You're helping now,' Miranda told her. 'Being able to talk about my plans to a trusted friend like you means that things become clearer in my mind.'

'We must keep in touch about this,' said June. 'Late evening is usually a good time to phone me. By then Amy is fast asleep. I never talk on the phone for long in the daytime, because it isn't fair on her. She needs me, and she can't possibly understand what I'm doing when I'm talking at a lump of plastic instead of focussing on her.'

Miranda chuckled. 'I've never thought of a phone like that before, but I see what you mean. If I were in Amy's position the whole thing would be incomprehensible.' Then her voice became serious. 'June, Amy is so lucky to have you as a mother.'

June shook her head. 'No, it's the other way round. I'm so lucky to have Amy.'

'Yes, of course, but what I'm getting at is how important it is to have a mother who has that level of understanding.'

'I certainly try. All the time I think about what it must be like to be tiny, and to be completely dependent, and I try to respond to that. Miranda, I've sometimes wondered if not being able to have a child sooner has been a blessing in disguise.'

'I hadn't thought about it like that. All I could see was how hard it was for you not to have the family that you had longed for. I was so happy for you when Amy was born.'

'Simon and I can see very clearly how much more mature we are now. And it isn't just that we're older. Somehow going through that long process of not knowing if I would ever become pregnant has led to us both valuing Amy even more. It taught us how to value a new human life.'

'I understand what you're saying.'

'I'm bound to make mistakes. Everyone does. But the difference is that I'm more likely to be able to see them and think about what to do about them, instead of just rushing on, assuming that everything's fine so long as Amy's growing bigger.'

94

'It's a huge responsibility,' Miranda reflected. 'I think I knew that when I was trying to help Mum with Amber and Jessica, but because I was so young myself, I couldn't have put it into words. The last few weeks have taught me that I don't have to worry about them any more, and that I must concentrate on myself.'

'I'm very glad to hear you say that.'

'June, you played a big part in the change in my thinking. I'm so grateful.'

'If it weren't for Amy being in my life, I don't think I would have seen your situation so clearly.' June finished the end of her row of knitting. 'I think I can hear her stirring. I must pop upstairs and check.'

Miranda enjoyed the rest of the day very much. She and June looked after Amy together. She was fascinated by all Amy's actions and responses. She noticed that there was a freshness about the experience – almost as if she had never been involved in the care of a baby before. She had planned to leave soon after Simon came in, but when the time came, she found that she could not tear herself away, and instead asked if she could stay on while Amy was having her bath.

'Of course,' said June. 'I'll make something for us all to eat, while you and Simon are upstairs with Amy.'

Surprise registered on Miranda's face.

Simon noticed this. 'Bathtime's usually my domain,' he explained with a grin. 'It's the high spot of my day.'

Miranda could tell that he really meant this. As he carried Amy upstairs, she noticed that she grabbed his nose in one tiny hand and dug her fingers into it.

'Ow!' he exclaimed in mock distress. Then he looked at Amy and made a noise like a quacking duck. Amy squealed with delight, and Simon only just managed to deflect her other hand before she poked a finger in his eye.

At the end of the evening, Simon insisted on giving Miranda a lift back to her house. Although she protested, he was adamant. June waved goodbye at the door.

'Remember to phone to let me know how things are going,' she called.

'I promise,' Miranda called back.

'And feel free to come and join us again soon,' Simon told her on the way. 'I trust you completely with Amy. Watching you with her leaves me thinking that you've already reared twins,' he joked.

Miranda smiled, but said nothing. She felt no need to inform him of her experiences of helping to rear Amber and Jessica.

Simon dropped her off outside her door, and waited until she was inside before driving off into the night. Miranda flopped down into a chair and shut her eyes. Now she could let all the memories of her anxieties about the care of Amber and Jessica wash over her and drain away. She felt exhausted, but it was a healthy feeling.

It was only later that she thought to check her mobile. There were a couple of texts. There was one from Mum, sending her love and hoping to speak soon. The other was from Kate: *Bruno's fine,* it read. Miranda stared at it for several minutes, perplexed. Then she realised what it meant, and laughed.

'No doubt I'll get the full story soon,' she murmured. 'And now, to bed.'

Chapter Eleven

Miranda slept very well that night, and when she woke she was brimming with energy. Straight away she remembered that her dreams had been full of colour and excited anticipation of things to come. She leapt out of bed and flung open the window, allowing icy air to pour into the room. She then found herself engaging in a routine of strenuous exercises, before prancing round her bedroom in a way that surprised her. When she caught sight of herself in the mirror, her movements reminded her strongly of what she had seen of flamenco dancing, and she resolved that she must find a way forward with that without delay.

Downstairs, she devoured a hearty breakfast and then planned her day. The evening would be taken up with phone conversations with her mum and with Kate. She chuckled when she thought of Kate. She was certain that the updates from her would be fascinating. Fleetingly she felt frustrated that there was no way of advancing contact with the college or with the Business Gateway at the moment, but there was so much that she could plan about other aspects of her business, which she knew would more than fill the day. It was so good to have the interest and support of her friends as well as her parents. Kate, June and Tess were clearly keen. She could bounce ideas off them in confidence, and she was sure that they would be willing to do a little research if she needed that.

The morning seemed to fly past. Internet searches revealed many avenues that she wanted to follow. She noted contact details of people to phone after the holiday break was over, together with a number of central questions on which to focus.

Before lunch, she went out to pick up some essential supplies from the local shop, taking with her a small notebook.

This turned out to be a very wise decision, because she was only a few minutes from her home when new ideas flooded into her mind, and she jotted them down as she walked. Thus absorbed, she had little awareness of anything else.

The shop appeared as if from nowhere, and she lingered outside for a few minutes to make more notes. Inside the shop she found it difficult to recall what she had come for, and it was in this state that she rounded the corner of a stand and bumped straight into Malcolm, who was carrying a basket that was overflowing. A pack of toilet rolls fell on to the floor, and he bent to retrieve it.

'Oops! Sorry,' Miranda apologised.

Malcolm grinned. 'Don't worry about that. I shouldn't have tried to put it all in one basket. It doesn't fit. It isn't all for me.'

Miranda noticed that she wasn't having any of the usual feelings about mud, and she lingered. 'Have you got someone staying over the holidays?'

'No, one of my neighbours isn't all that well, and I offered to get some things in for her.'

'That's kind of you.'

Malcolm went on. 'She's generally quite sprightly, and I don't want her slipping on an icy patch and breaking her hip or something.'

'How old is she?'

'Must be in her eighties, I should think.'

'A friend of mine is moving in straight after New Year,' Miranda told him.

Malcolm stared at her blankly, and then said, 'Oh, that's nice. I hope it goes well.' He turned away and concentrated on a shelf of preserves.

Miranda felt puzzled. Malcolm had finished the conversation rather abruptly. No, it was as if he had severed it. She felt a little irked. She had been able to relate to him in a more normal way, and he had cut off from her. She had an impulse to tap him on the shoulder and ask him what was the matter, but thought better of it, and instead focussed her mind on what she needed to buy.

At the checkout, she was next but one behind Malcolm. She could see that his face was set, and that he was in a hurry to get out of the shop. She saw no sign of him when she left the shop, and wandered back home slowly, concentrating on selecting a name for her business.

'*Wedding Aspirations...* or maybe *Wedding Inspirations*,' she murmured. '*Knotty Problems...*' No, definitely not that, she thought. '*The Big Day... Wedding Support...* No, that's too stuffy. *Wedding Solutions...*' She put down her shopping and scribbled in her notebook, promising herself that she would speak to the others soon to get their views.

As she neared her house, her thoughts returned to the strange encounter with Malcolm. There had been two unusual things about it. The first was her own lack of concern about mud and any other perceived downsides of his appearance, and the second was his odd reaction when she told him that Kate was coming to stay. Perhaps if she had perceived him in the usual muddy way, his odd reaction would never have come to light.

'Maybe I should stick with the mud,' she muttered crossly as she opened her front door. 'And I suppose I ought to tell Kate about this.'

Her irritability dissolved instantly when the phone rang and she answered it to find it was her mother calling.

'Mum!' she exclaimed joyfully. 'I've got so much to talk to you about.'

'Then I'm glad I didn't wait until this evening, dear. I was going to leave a message to say I've sent off those photos.'

'That's great! I've been thinking about Granny Ann so much, and when the photos arrive I'll put them all round the house. I've told Kate about her, and I'm sure she'll be interested to see them.'

'And now tell me your news,' her mother directed.

Miranda began to speak, and quickly found that she could

not stop. She went from subject to subject without a break, while her mother listened quietly.

'Mum, are you still there?' Miranda asked anxiously. Glancing at her watch she realised that half an hour had passed.

'Of course I'm here,' her mother replied kindly. 'I'm so interested in what you're saying, and I didn't want to interrupt.'

'But say something now!' Miranda ordered. Her hand flew to her mouth. 'Mum, I'm sorry. I shouldn't speak like that. I don't know what's happening to me these days.'

'I think a lot of good is happening. This time away from office work is turning out to be the right thing for you. Now, give me a moment or two to assemble my thoughts.'

'I'm not trying to rush you,' Miranda assured her anxiously.

Her mother laughed. 'You can try if you want, but I can only go at my speed.'

Miranda was greatly reassured by this, and waited.

'The first thing I want to say is that I'm terribly sorry I wasn't able to help you when Granny Ann died. I felt completely lost myself, and nearly straight away I became pregnant with Amber, and started feeling very sick. That time must have been awful for you, yet as soon as Amber was born you tried your best to help with her.'

'But...'

'You've told me that you were comforted by holding Amber,' said her mother. 'I can understand that now you point it out to me, and I wish I'd seen it for myself at the time.'

Miranda felt as if something inside her was unravelling.

Her mother went on. 'Your dress designs sound stunning. I only wish your father and I had realised that you had such aptitude. We could have encouraged you to study art and design. Well, it's certainly not too late to help you with this.'

'I...'

Her mother continued determinedly. 'You mentioned flamenco dancing.'

'Did I?' asked Miranda weakly.

'Yes, you certainly did. There's plenty of colour, fire and

personal expression in that. No wonder you felt attracted by it. I only wish you'd told me when you were fourteen. I could certainly have fixed something up for you.'

'But Amber and Jessica...'

'There would have been time and resources,' her mother interjected firmly. 'The trouble was that after Granny Ann's death you stopped trying to get anything for yourself.'

'Maybe...'

'It wasn't your fault. Your father and I should have seen what was happening. Miranda, I'm sorry if I sound forceful, but I feel very strongly about all of this. Now that I see you beginning to blossom, I feel sad that it couldn't have happened earlier, and I've clearly had a part to play in the delay.'

'Don't feel badly, Mum,' Miranda pleaded.

'It's right that I have regrets,' her mother insisted. 'Now, tell me more about Malcolm. What did you tell him about Kate?'

Miranda was mystified. Why was her mother going over this again? 'I told him that a friend was moving in with me very soon.'

Her mother chuckled. 'Then I think I know why he suddenly turned away.'

'Why?'

'He probably thought you had a boyfriend moving in, and was feeling a bit jealous.'

'Oh no! I never intended him to think that.'

'Of course you didn't.'

'I don't like to think of him as someone who's feeling jealous. *And I don't want him to have that kind of feeling around me!*' Miranda finished emphatically.

'Well, I'm sure that when you introduce him to Kate, he'll realise his mistake.'

'*That's not the point! He's not a potential boyfriend of mine!*'

At this, Miranda's mother recognised that her daughter was in a kind of panic. Attempting to calm her, she said, 'It's all right, dear. I do understand. You said earlier that you'd like to come out to see us with Kate for a long weekend. Come as soon as you can.'

The uncomfortable thoughts about Malcolm dispersed instantly. 'I'll talk to Kate and we'll sort out some dates,' Miranda promised.

It was the middle of the afternoon when Kate made contact. Miranda was again deeply engrossed in dress design when she rang.

'I don't want to disturb you if you're doing something,' Kate began.

'Cut the cackle and give me the news.'

'Oof! That's pretty direct. Well, I'll take it at face value. I'll give you a précis first, and then you can decide whether or not you want more detail.'

'Okay.'

'Bruno and I are best of friends, and Nigel's fixed up a whole list of contacts for me about the dog walking. I'm wondering about *Whistle and I'll Come* for a business name.'

Miranda started to laugh, and for several minutes the friends were unable to speak.

'We're going to have to do some brainstorming in this arena,' said Miranda, although she was finding it difficult to speak properly. 'I've been trying to put something together for my business name, but I'm not convinced I've got there yet.'

'Okay, I'll put it on the agenda for when I move in.' Kate paused for a moment, and then asked, 'Would you mind if I go to a party with Nigel tonight?'

'Why on earth did you think you had to ask me?'

'It's New Year's Eve.'

Miranda laughed. 'I'd almost forgotten. My head's so full of business plans. I've an open invitation to go round to June and Simon's. I'll probably give them a ring and fix to pop round for a couple of hours.'

That seemed to satisfy Kate. 'Any other news?' she asked.

'I had a long talk with Mum. Well, I talked *at* her for ages. I think I covered everything I could think of. She was great.'

'How did she react to the thing about cuddling Amber?'

'She couldn't have been better. And she brought in other things about it as well. Kate, I told her we're hoping to go out and see her and Dad for a long weekend soon.'

'Sounds good. I'm certainly up for spending some of my meagre savings on the flights. When shall we aim for?'

'I thought we could decide once you're installed here.'

'Put it on the list, together with the "business names dilemma". Miranda, is there anything else before I ring off?'

'Er… Maybe I ought to mention about Malcolm.'

'You've seen him again already? What happened?' asked Kate quickly.

'Before I say anything, I'd better warn you that this is a very sensitive subject. I was pretty jumpy with Mum about it on the phone, and I'm not sure yet what it's all about.'

'Maybe you fancy him, but don't want to admit it,' Kate guessed.

'If you were here, I think I might be tempted to hit you with one of my large cushions,' said Miranda through gritted teeth.

'Why not just tell me what happened, and we can take it from there?'

As Miranda progressed through the story, Kate hooted with laughter at the possibility that Malcolm had assumed that she was a lover. 'I can't wait to see his face when you introduce me.'

'I'll have to hide you so you can't come out with anything that'll get me in even deeper water,' Miranda told her.

'The deep water is already inside you,' Kate reminded her soberly. 'Miranda, I know we've made progress, but I think we've both still got quite a long way to go.'

Chapter Twelve

Kate's move went very smoothly. Miranda had offered to go and help her to bring her belongings across, but Kate had ordered a taxi, and arrived in the late afternoon with a number of bags and cases. Together they organised everything, and then made something to eat. After that they sat and chatted for a long time.

'How did the party go?' asked Miranda.

'It was great for business,' Kate replied. 'I went round as many people as I could. I soon discovered it's a shame I haven't got business cards yet, but I wrote my name and mobile number into at least ten diaries. That should harvest something.'

Miranda was deeply impressed that Kate had used the party in this way, and said so.

'It's no good putting things off. That was my last day of pay from our former employer. Now I'm sailing into the unknown.' Kate finished with a dramatic gesture.

'Why don't we design your business cards this evening?' asked Miranda.

'Mm… I'd like to do that, but I don't want to take time away from your own planning.'

'It's going to be a while before I'll be ready to design cards for myself, but going through the process of doing yours is going to help.'

'I hadn't thought about that angle,' Kate mused.

'Let's at least make a start.'

'Okay. I'll need my name, my mobile number and the business name, together with a kind of mission statement thing.'

'It'll be a good idea to collect some testimonials,' Miranda pointed out.

'But I can't collect them until I'm working with dogs.'

'Do you think Nigel might write one for you?'

'I hadn't thought of that. Yes, I think he might. I'm sure Bruno would like to help, but unfortunately he can't write.'

They played around with advertising ideas for a while, but could not come to any final conclusion. Nothing seemed quite right.

'We'll have to sleep on it,' Kate decided. 'Perhaps something will come to me in a dream. Ah! What about *"Doggy Heaven – experienced dog walker available: cost will suit your purse"*?'

Miranda kicked Kate playfully. Then she became thoughtful. 'Maybe a business card isn't the best idea. Shall we design a leaflet instead? You could include a lot more information, and we could produce some on my computer.'

'Hey, that's a great idea! Can you give me something to write on?'

Miranda passed her some paper, and Kate worked for a while with an intense expression on her face. Miranda picked up her sketch pad and continued working on a dress design.

Some time later, Kate raised her head and said, 'I think I've got a draft together now.'

'Tell me what you've decided.'

'It's not finished. I suddenly realised that I don't have to stick to dog walking, so I've put on the front "Petcare in your own home. Affordable support for your pets while you're at work." '

'Sounds good. Read on.'

'I've got my name and mobile number there. Inside will be a list of things I can do. That will include dog walking, of course. And the final section should be about qualifications and experience, together with testimonials.' Kate pulled a face and added, 'Unfortunately I haven't got any of those things yet.'

Miranda became very businesslike. 'You'll need to do some research. I'll jot down some ideas.' She took out her notebook and made a list: RSPCA, police dog handlers, council dog warden, dog obedience classes, local vet. 'These are only ideas, but you might get some leads from some of them. And you might be able to get some voluntary work for a few weeks that will produce testimonials.'

'You're absolutely amazing!' Kate exclaimed. 'I'll get on with this tomorrow. And I can start with some simple flyers, but update them as I get more information.'

It was when Miranda went to the shop the next day to stock up on their dwindling food supplies that she saw a new notice had appeared on the pegboard on the wall. She was in the habit of glancing through what was there, to see when anything new was added. The notice was a little larger than postcard size, and merely said: *Potential office space available locally.* It gave a mobile number, and a name – Mr M Hurst. On impulse, she jotted down the details in her notebook, collected her shopping, and returned home, where she found Kate still hard at work.

'Do you fancy a break?' she asked.

Kate glanced at her watch. 'I could do with a drink, but I've still got quite a lot to cover, so I mustn't be long.'

As they sipped hot tea together, Miranda told Kate about the new advertisement.

'Why are you interested?' asked Kate. 'You don't need office space.'

'I might. And if all goes well, I'll need somewhere to see clients.'

'Can't you do all that on the phone or e-mail?'

'I could, but it wouldn't have the same quality of personal touch. Ideally I need something that looks and feels like a living room.'

'If I weren't here, you could do it from home.'

'Not with my staircase,' Miranda pointed out. 'And anyway, I wouldn't want people clomping up it to my bathroom. Kate, it might seem a bit premature, but I'm going to give this number a ring and find out what's available.'

Kate sat quietly while Miranda went ahead.

A voice answered almost immediately. 'Malcolm Hurst

speaking.'

Miranda's face went bright red, and she put the phone down very quickly.

'Kate, it's Malcolm!'

'You'd better speak to him,' Kate advised. 'He'll know it's this number that called.'

'No, he won't. I pressed 141 first, and even if I hadn't, he wouldn't know this was my number.' Miranda felt curiously breathless, and was having to force herself to speak.

'What's the matter?' asked Kate, concerned.

'I don't know. I just don't know...' Miranda's voice trailed off into a kind of wail.

'You must have some idea,' Kate pressed gently.

Miranda put her head in her hands, and then said in muffled tones, 'It could be that I'm trying to consider having something to do with him, but really I'm too scared.'

'That's a bit convoluted, but I think I follow what you're saying. Do you know what's scaring you?'

The muffled voice went on. 'I think it's something to do with passion. I won't know what to do with it if I have it. It's all very well having it about dress designs. It feels great then – completely natural and real – but I don't have to cope with a person at the same time.'

'But I thought you were phoning that number about a possible business arrangement.'

Miranda sat bolt upright. 'Kate, thank you so much! I'd forgotten that. Let me take a few deep breaths, and then I'll try again.'

Kate marvelled at the apparent ease with which Miranda made the call.

'Malcolm, it's Miranda ... Yes, I phoned a few minutes ago, but I was interrupted. I saw your card in the shop ... Yes, office space ... I'd like to see it ... Tomorrow would suit me very well ... I'll see you then.' She rang off.

'That sounded fine,' Kate remarked.

Miranda did not respond to this, except to say, 'I'm going

there for half past two, and I'll ring the Business Gateway before that to see if I can set up a meeting soon. I've checked the college website again, and I should be able to speak to someone tomorrow.'

'I've been following up some of the suggestions you made yesterday,' Kate announced, 'and I've got some appointments fixed over the next few days. I feel really positive about it all. Oh, and Nigel sent me a text inviting me out to dinner next week.'

'Are you going?'

'How could I turn him down? This is an ideal opportunity to wear my robin earrings,' Kate replied flippantly. Then she continued. 'Joking apart, I'm feeling a bit edgy. Going out for dinner is a step up from visiting Bruno.'

'You've got to go ahead with this,' Miranda urged earnestly. 'I'll help you all I can. From what you've told me, he comes across as a really nice person. And his sister's in your flat, and she seems okay as well. The signs are good.'

Kate looked Miranda straight in the eye. 'Plague,' she said deliberately.

'What on earth do you mean?' asked Miranda. She felt quite offended. She was doing her best to encourage Kate to connect with Nigel, and all she was getting was criticism.

'Oh, Miranda... You're very kind and supportive to me about the thing with Nigel, but we can't concentrate on that and forget about your situation.'

'But I'm talking a lot about my business,' Miranda objected.

'And mine,' Kate reminded her gently. 'Look, I noticed that when you phoned Malcolm in "businesswoman mode" you were completely fine, but before that you were all over the place.'

Miranda was obstinate. 'Maybe I don't like him.'

'Maybe so, but that wouldn't be a reason for getting in a state.'

Miranda considered this, but she felt that Kate was putting

undue pressure on her, and said so.

'Miranda, the pressure isn't from me. It's from the feelings you're trying to hide from yourself.' Kate clapped her hand to her mouth. She was astonished by what had come out of it. She certainly hadn't planned to say something like that. However, she was glad to discover that it had had the desired effect of getting through to Miranda.

'Kate, you're so wise,' Miranda said appreciatively. 'When you put it like that, I can see straight away what you mean.'

Kate grinned. 'I'm not so sure that I understand it completely, but it sounds right.'

'I think what I've got to do is get to grips with the fear of feeling passionate when someone else is around.'

Kate was impressed by her friend's honesty. 'Do you feel frightened about it when I'm around?'

Miranda dismissed the idea. 'Of course not!'

'Do you feel frightened about it when you're with June and Simon?'

'No...'

'But when Malcolm's around...'

Miranda flushed. 'That's quite different... unless it's to do with a business proposition.'

'My diagnosis is that you fancy him,' said Kate bluntly.

'I don't! I can't... I...' Miranda was struggling.

'I'm a fine one to talk all knowledgeably about this subject,' Kate reminded her, 'but I think you ought to know that it's okay to fancy someone but not do anything about it.'

'You mean... just have the feelings... privately?'

'Yes. Well, and tell a close friend about it... if you want to.'

Relief flooded through Miranda's body, and she felt exhausted. Although she was now quite limp, she liked the feeling of relaxing completely like this.

Kate decided that now was the time to change the subject. 'We haven't yet picked dates for going out to see your folks.'

Miranda surprised her by saying, 'Can we leave that for

now? I need to get to the bottom of this mess I'm in.'

'We might not find it today,' Kate warned.

'But I want to try,' said Miranda determinedly. She sat up straight. 'Now, before Granny Ann died, I was the only child in a close, warm, loving family. When she died, I was suddenly in a state of shock, and so was my mum. And before we could do anything with that, Mum was pregnant…'

'Mm…' Kate mused. 'There's certainly a saying "when one life ends, another begins." '

'… and soon she started feeling really really sick.'

Kate continued. 'So, by the time she was feeling better from that, Amber was nearly ready to be born, and no one had noticed that you were struggling with everything.'

Miranda looked at Kate appreciatively. 'Correct. Then I saw my mum and dad cuddling Amber, I copied them, and all the horrible feelings seemed to melt away. Mum got pregnant again, she needed help with Amber while she was being sick, Jessica was born, and then I had two babies to cuddle.'

'And you kept on cuddling them – first physically, and then in other ways – until pretty recently…'

'… so that I wouldn't have to think about how awful it was to lose the feeling that Granny Ann, Mum and Dad were all there for me, whenever I wanted.'

Kate let out a long breath. 'We got hold of some of this before, but there's much more here. I can see it as if it were happening in front of me right now. No wonder you have such difficulty with passionate feelings. Oh, Miranda, I promise I'll never try to push you about Malcolm, or anyone else, ever again.'

Miranda was horrified. 'But you must!'

'Surely that would be really cruel?'

'It would be far worse if you didn't,' said Miranda flatly. 'I'd be doomed to go through my life avoiding thinking about it all. I'd get wonderful wedding dresses made for everyone else, and never have one for myself.'

'When you put it like that…'

'There's no other way,' Miranda finished emphatically. 'Can you spare some time now or this evening, so that I can talk through my impending visit to Malcolm and his office space? And I don't mean only from a business angle.'

Kate was about to reply, but then she stopped and considered. She felt strongly that she should continue to talk about what she and Miranda had begun, but at the same time she knew that she must finish the work she had started. She had intended only to take a short break, and this had already extended to well over half an hour.

Eventually she took a deep breath and said, 'I feel really torn between this and what I was doing before, and I don't know what to do.'

'Then the decision's easy. We'll both get on with work now.'

'I'll need at least a couple of hours,' said Kate uncertainly.

'After that we'll eat, and then we can talk. That's if you've got any energy left.'

'There'll be no question about that,' Kate assured her. 'I'm finding that planning my future work is *giving* me energy rather than using it up.'

Chapter Thirteen

Miranda felt calm and well prepared as she approached Malcolm's market garden. She and Kate had sat up quite late, deep in discussion about it. This morning she had made an appointment with the Business Gateway for next week, and she had found out from the college everything else she needed to know before booking the courses she wanted.

It wasn't quite half past two, so she walked a few hundred yards further along the road, before turning and heading straight for the building. Malcolm opened the door instantly, and she could only surmise that he had been watching out for her arrival.

'Come into the office,' he invited. 'I've had the heater on.'

The modestly sized room was snug and warm, so Miranda took off her coat, and Malcolm hung it behind the door.

He pointed to a battered leather-covered chair. 'Take a seat. I'll get behind my desk.'

Miranda took a folder from her bag. 'I have a list of questions here. I'm sure if we start talking most of the answers will emerge.'

'I thought I'd begin by telling you what this building's being used for at the moment. Apart from this office, there are a couple of rooms I live in, a smallish room that's filled mainly with junk, and there's a large store at the back. I was thinking of emptying the junk room and moving my bed in there. That would mean I could change the room that's my bedroom now into my sitting room, and thus free up the front room for let.'

'Won't that leave you a bit cramped?'

Malcolm shook his head. 'Should be fine. I'll show you round, and you'll see. Freeing up the front room is the best option. As you'll have noticed, it's got quite a nice bay window, so potential customers can see what they're coming to.' He stood up. 'Come and see.'

Miranda followed him, and found herself in a well-proportioned room with an interesting cornice. This, together with the design of the bay window and the substantial skirting boards, gave the room the appearance of being solid and lasting. Mentally she noted that it would need repainting, the floor covering must be replaced, and good curtains would make the window look even better. The light fitting was attractive. Her eyes moved to the fireplace. The surround looked entirely in keeping with the room, and she thought it must be the original one.

'The chimney works,' Malcolm informed her. 'I have a log fire most evenings, but if I need the room in the daytime, I have an electric heater.'

Miranda shivered.

'Come back into the warm,' Malcolm said quickly.

Seated in the office, Miranda explained her situation. 'Seeing your card got me thinking. My business isn't up and running yet, but once it is, I'll need somewhere suitable to see clients. With appropriate refurbishment, your front room appears to be ideal.'

'I put the card up to see if there was any local interest. I didn't want to move all my things around only to discover that there were no takers. My plan would be to be out of it by Easter, although I could make it earlier.'

'At this stage, I can't say when I would need something,' Miranda told him. 'How much will it cost per month?'

Malcolm looked uncomfortable. 'I need to do some research to find out the going rate in this area. Of course, I should have done that before I put the card up.' He cleared his throat nervously. 'If you want to go ahead, I would waive the first couple of months' rent if you took responsibility for the refurbishment.'

'Malcolm, are you sure? That's a very generous offer.'

'Spring's a very busy time for me. I won't want to be tied up with painting and the like.' He stopped, and then added hurriedly, 'Although I'd give you a hand whenever I could.'

'Perhaps we both need to think this through, and then have another conversation,' Miranda stated firmly. 'I'd like to say I'll take it, but I don't know how long it will take me to pull everything together so that I can accept clients.'

'I can be flexible.'

'What if someone else comes to look at the room?'

Malcolm looked straight at her. 'I'll walk down the road with you, and when I get to the shop, I'll take my card down.'

Until now Miranda had felt fine, but at this moment she began to feel very uncomfortable. 'Surely you should wait and see what other options emerge,' she began.

'I've changed my mind,' he said determinedly. 'I'll let it if you want it, but if not, I'll probably wait for another year.'

Miranda tried again. 'Why not leave it that if someone else contacts you, you'll phone me to give me first refusal?'

Malcolm shook his head. 'Do you want to see the rest before you leave?'

'I don't think so, except perhaps the bathroom facilities.'

'Of course.'

He led the way down a short passage, and opened the door into a nicely decorated shower room with a toilet and a washhand basin.

Miranda was so taken by surprise that she gasped involuntarily. 'It's lovely!'

'Glad you like it. I had some spare time in November.' He mentioned this with a casual air. 'I had to make a start somewhere. All the rooms could do with some paint at the very least. And if you want to see the kitchen area, I think I'll have to say no.'

'I'll get my coat.'

'Okay. I'll be with you in a minute.'

They left the building together, and Malcolm locked the door behind him.

Kate was out when Miranda got back to the house, but she had left a note to say that she would be in around seven. Miranda longed to tell someone about the day's events, and her hand lingered over the phone for a moment or two. But it was too early to phone June, and Tess was probably out. She went to put the kettle on, but did not get as far as filling it before she decided to ring her mother.

Her mother was clearly delighted to hear her. 'I'm so glad you phoned. I was thinking of calling you. I was wondering how things were going.'

Miranda needed no further prompting, and she poured out everything she had realised about the source of her difficulties with Malcolm. This led to a lengthy discussion, after which she went on to tell of her visit to his office, and the possible use of a room. Her mother listened intently, making no comment until she had finished.

'This is a very interesting opportunity indeed. I can already imagine the final result – an inviting place with a comfortable sofa, a couple of occasional chairs, and a teamaker discreetly in one corner. Is there room for parking?'

'Yes, there's no problem about that.'

'And with it being a front room, an appropriate sign in the window will assure clients that they have come to the right place.'

'I'll have to paint the hallway, too. It's a bit of a mess at the moment.'

'Miranda, I can't wait to tell your dad. He'll want to jump on the next plane to come and make a start for you.'

Miranda was horrified. 'No! He mustn't do that. I'm not sure yet about taking it. It's going to depend on so many things, and much of that is to do with setting up all my business links. It's going to take ages for me to do that properly. And I don't want to end up with a situation where I've got a beautiful room and no clients to come and see me in it.'

'Don't worry,' her mother soothed. 'I'll make sure he doesn't come. Well, not yet.'

Thus reassured, Miranda went on to tell her mother about

the impending meeting at the Business Gateway, and the conversation she'd had with the person at the college.

'You've been very busy. I'm impressed. And before we ring off, tell me how Kate is getting on.'

'She's forging ahead with ideas, and she's bound to have clients long before I do.'

'That's to be expected. There's a lot less preparation involved.'

'She'll feel much better when she's got some money coming in. Oh, and she's going out to dinner next week with someone called Nigel who she met at the letting agency.' Miranda chuckled. 'She's planning to wear the robin earrings I bought her for Christmas.'

Chapter Fourteen

A whole week went by in a flash. Miranda and Kate were determined to push things forward, and every day they made more progress. Thursday evening was Kate's dinner date with Nigel. Kate and Miranda had set aside Friday evening to catch up with everything. It turned out that Kate's 'night out' on Thursday took up most of Friday as well, so by the time she got back to Miranda's house, it was time to make something to eat and then settle down to talk. Neither of them felt particularly hungry, so they made a few sandwiches, and then began.

'We've hardly spoken all week,' Miranda remarked.

'Yes, either one of us has been out at a meeting, or we've had our heads down, working our socks off.'

'Let's start with you spilling the beans about last night.'

'There aren't any beans to spill. The food was nice, and Nigel liked my earrings. I told him how I came by them, and he told me his sister really likes being in my flat. We spent much of the evening honing my plans. He's pretty astute, and he came out with some helpful things. He gave me a list of a few more people who are interested in using my services. When it was time to leave, he said he'd made up the bed in the spare room in case I wanted to stay over. I was about to decline, but then he mentioned that he had some silly night clothes that I could borrow, and I decided I'd go for it.'

Miranda was curious. 'What were the clothes like?'

'I wished you were there to see. You'd have died laughing. There was a pyjama top and bottom made out of white material with huge black spots. They were so baggy that I looked like a clown. And to top it all, there was a matching Wee Willie Winkie nightcap.'

Miranda started to splutter.

'I knew you'd like that,' said Kate, 'so I got Nigel to take a photo of me on my mobile.' She reached into her bag, and handed it to Miranda.

'The sight of you like this is side-splitting.' Miranda shook with mirth. When she had recovered sufficiently to be able to speak again, she said, 'I'm going to print this photo. Who knows, I might get clients who want something more interesting than a lacy negligée!'

'I never thought of that. Miranda, maybe you're about to make a fortune with a new genre of the ideal wedding wardrobe.'

At this, both began to giggle uncontrollably.

It was Miranda who recovered first. 'We'd better settle down soon and talk about the more serious things.'

'Okay. What have you been up to?' asked Kate.

'I'm starting two short courses at the college next week. They're very part time, so I'll be able to keep on with everything else. The Business Gateway people were very nice, and they wished me well, but I didn't find them particularly inspiring.'

'That's what I've heard from other people, but I didn't say anything because I didn't want to put you off.'

'You were right,' said Miranda. 'It's best for me to find out for myself.'

'How are you doing with the "Malcolm" thing?' asked Kate.

'Do you mean Malcolm himself, or what he represents?'

'Both, I suppose.'

'Well, I haven't had any more contact with him, but I've been thinking a lot about the accommodation, and what it might be like being around his place.'

'Sounds like a good sign.'

'I thought so. Kate, have you spoken to your mum recently?'

'No, but I've sent a few texts to let her know how things are going.'

'I bet she's pleased.'

'That's a bit of an understatement. And she keeps egging me on. I find that really helpful. She asked after you.'

'And my mum keeps asking after you.'

'It's great getting all this encouragement,' said Kate.

'We're very lucky with that. And I've spoken to Tess again this week.'

Kate pulled a face.

'Kate, she was extremely positive and helpful about what I'm doing.'

'I'm glad to hear it, but I'm still wary on your behalf. I think she's quite capable of swamping you if she feels like it.'

'I know what you mean, but I'm certain she's changing.'

'Have you heard anything from your sisters?'

'Nothing. Sometimes I feel sad about it, but mostly I hardly think about them. That surprises me.'

'I'm convinced you're going in the right direction. This is the route to stopping being an extra mother, and ending up as a sister.'

'Yes, I really feel that now. At first I could see it as a concept, but I struggled with my feelings.'

'Miranda, I've got an announcement to make.'

'You're engaged?'

Kate kicked her gently. 'Don't be silly. Of course not. I'm seeing my first client on Monday morning.'

'Congratulations!' exclaimed Miranda. She clasped Kate's hand in hers and gave it a squeeze. 'It's so exciting! Tell me who it is.'

'I'm going to make friends with an elderly dog that belongs to a woman who's going to be in hospital for a couple of days the following week. She feels the dog couldn't cope with kennels or being in someone else's house, however kind the people were. The dog's used to pottering around the house and garden, and not doing much else. She thinks he'll be fine if I go in and pat him and feed him each day. After seeing him, I've got a booking in the afternoon for a cat, and then something each day except Friday. And I've got my first batch of leaflets printed up. I've started handing them round, and I left a pile with Nigel.'

'Oh, let me have a look,' said Miranda eagerly.

Kate passed her one from her bag, and Miranda studied it carefully.

'These look very professional. There's just one thing.'

'What's that?'

'You don't need an apostrophe in "rabbits." '

Kate was annoyed with herself.

'I wouldn't worry. I don't suppose anyone will notice. What they're really bothered about is whether or not you're going to turn up and do what you've promised.'

'True, but I'm going to correct it before I print off the next batch of leaflets.'

'Who's Adrian Simmons in the testimonials section?'

'He's next door to Nigel. You know... the dog-share system for Bruno.'

'Oh, right.' Miranda paused, and then said, 'Actually, I have to admit to feeling a bit envious.'

'Don't worry about that. No doubt I'll soon be feeling envious of *you*.'

'Anyway, I got some samples of materials through the post this week. Do you want to see them? I think they're beautiful.'

The next twenty minutes were spent looking at them, and discussing their qualities, merits and uses.

'Have you linked up with any dressmakers yet?'

'So far I've found one definite and two possibles.'

'That's good going.'

'Kate...'

'I'm all ears.'

'Would you think I was completely mad if I went ahead with Malcolm's place soon? I could get Dad to come over and help me with the refurbishment while I keep advancing my research and doing my courses.'

Kate thought for a while before replying. Then she said slowly, 'From what you've told me, the only money you stand to lose is what you spend on furniture, curtains, paint and floor covering. That's in the unlikely event that you never see any clients there.'

'I'm really keen.'

Kate saw that Miranda's cheeks were flushed, and that she looked vibrant. Kate pointed to the phone. 'Why not speak to your dad right now?'

Miranda hesitated only for a moment. Then she grabbed the phone.

When she rang off, she turned to Kate and said, 'I don't know if you got the gist of it, but I spoke to Dad, and he's going to talk things over with Mum. He's got it in mind that they'll both come across if I give Malcolm the go-ahead for that room.' She hugged herself. 'I'd so like them both to be involved. Dad's going to look at flights and see what accommodation there is around here.'

Kate fell silent for a moment before saying quietly, 'If I weren't here, they could stay with you.'

Miranda answered firmly. 'No, Dad was clear that he fancied a challenge, and finding somewhere different for him and Mum is part of it. And besides, they really like it that you're here with me.'

Kate relaxed.

Miranda went on. 'I've been wondering if I'm being a bit too ambitious about the business, at least for now. More and more I'm thinking that to begin with I might concentrate on female wedding attire, innovative gifts, and unusual buffet choices. I've collected together an enormous amount of information about these areas already. I think I'll feel overstretched if I'm trying to do complete wedding plans as well.'

'But maybe you should add venues to your initial list.'

'You're right. I've got a couple of promising ones already...'

Kate started to giggle.

Miranda felt irritated. 'What's so amusing?' she asked

stiffly.

'Perhaps Malcolm can show your clients round the parsnips...'

Miranda saw the funny side of this, and started to giggle, too.

By Sunday, it had been decided that Miranda would contact Malcolm the next day, to let him know that she was taking the room.

'Why don't we walk up there this afternoon?' Kate suggested. 'I'd like to see where it is.'

Miranda hesitated.

'Go on,' Kate pressed.

'Er... I'm feeling a bit edgy about the idea.'

Kate was sympathetic. 'That's not surprising, given everything you've been going through.'

At this, Miranda felt less tense. 'Maybe we could walk up the road together, and if I start feeling ghastly we could go somewhere else instead.'

'That sounds like a good compromise, but if we have to abort the mission, we should try to work out exactly what's happening for you.'

Miranda could see the sense in this. 'It's a good thing it's Sunday, and we're not trying to push on with anything else. Otherwise I'm not sure I could try.'

Soon they were heading in the direction of the road that led to Malcolm's market garden.

'We've made so much progress in the last few weeks,' Kate reflected, 'and I feel quite optimistic about the future now. I was in a pretty bad state before, and trying desperately to cover it up.'

'You did a pretty good job of hiding it,' Miranda commented, 'whereas I didn't do so well. I ended up trying to hide the whole of me!'

'Never mind about that. We're not out of the woods yet, but we're well on our way.'

By this time they were passing the local shop. On impulse, Miranda stopped and went in, with Kate following close behind.

'What are you getting?' she asked.

'I want to check if Malcolm really did take that notice down,' Miranda said in a low voice. She scrutinised the notice board, and then checked around it.

Kate searched as well. 'Can't see anything.'

Miranda's shoulders relaxed. 'It's definitely gone. I was worried in case he hadn't stuck to the agreement, and I ended up looking like a fool.'

Kate gave her arm a squeeze. 'I don't think Malcolm sounds like that kind of person.'

As they left the shop, Miranda said quietly, 'I think I feel okay now about showing you where his place is.'

'We can still take it in stages,' Kate reminded her.

However, Miranda's confidence now seemed restored, and her pace quickened.

'Hey, wait for me!' said Kate playfully.

Miranda strode ahead. 'You'll see it on the right, round the next bend in the road.'

When it came into view, Miranda noticed straight away that Malcolm's van was not in its usual place. She felt a curious mixture of relief and disappointment.

'The window of my room is to the right of the front door,' she told Kate.

'Nice,' Kate observed. 'Pity I can't peer in.'

Miranda felt a lurch of panic. 'You mustn't!'

'I wasn't going to. I only said…'

'I know,' Miranda acknowledged. 'I panicked.'

'Do you think he's around?'

'His van's not there.'

'Well, we've accomplished our mission, so I'll take a photo, and then we'll go somewhere else,' Kate decided.

Miranda guided Kate along some interesting pathways, and by the time they returned home, it was dark.

Sipping from her mug of hot tea, Miranda suddenly asked,

'What's the next step with Nigel?'

'I thought we were concentrating on you and Malcolm,' said Kate defensively.

'Plague!' Miranda interjected.

'Fair cop... The truth is, I don't know.'

'What do you want it to be?'

'I'm enjoying the friendship, and I don't want to rock that boat.'

'That sounds a bit like me.' Miranda fell silent for a while, and then surprised herself by saying, 'We'd better plan our next moves.'

'That's a daring statement.'

'Well,' said Miranda, 'we could rehearse something and see what it feels like.'

'That sounds more feasible.' Kate grinned. 'You first.'

'No, you.'

This resulted in a burst of laughter, and it took some time before it eventually faded enough to allow conversation again.

'I've got a good idea,' Kate began. 'I'll decide the next step for you, and then you work one out for me.'

Miranda was quite taken with this idea, and agreed.

Kate shut her eyes, and wrinkled up her nose in concentration. After a while, she said in a strange voice, 'I can see it now...'

'Don't be silly, Kate,' Miranda told her. 'It's bad enough to think of the next step without you making it sound like a psychic game.'

Kate apologised. 'Sorry, I thought it might help. Seriously though, what's in my mind is tomorrow's contact with Malcolm.'

'It's very much in my mind, too. One part of me has no worries about it, but another part is freaking out.'

'That's the bit we've got to get a handle on. Miranda, how would you react if he suggested doing something together that wasn't about the business?'

'That's just it,' Miranda replied miserably. 'I think I'd

dematerialise.'

'How about saying "that's a nice idea" followed by "let's celebrate once my room's ready for action." That would put the whole thing off for several weeks.'

Miranda considered this. 'The first bit's all right, but the second bit needs a change. I can't talk about my room being ready for action. It sounds far too suggestive. Perhaps I could say "once I've got things up and running." '

'I agree to that amendment. Now turn the heat on me.'

Imitating what Kate had done, Miranda shut her eyes and screwed up her nose.

'Oh, stop it!' Kate commanded. 'You look ridiculous.'

'I wish you could have seen yourself when you did it,' Miranda told her calmly.

'Okay, okay,' said Kate crossly. 'Get on with the torture.'

'I don't want to torture you. I only want to help.'

'I know that. It's just that this whole process is really difficult.'

'You're telling me! Now, back to the point. Nigel took you out for dinner...'

'More correctly, he suggested that we had dinner together, but I insisted on paying for myself.'

'But he invited you to stay over, and he made it okay for you.'

Kate nodded mutely. Her feelings of anxiety were rising well past the point of discomfort. 'Hurry up.'

'So it's your turn to suggest something next time,' Miranda concluded.

Kate made a strangled sound, before taking a breath and saying quietly, 'I know.'

'Do you want me to think of something?'

Again Kate nodded.

'How about a nice long walk one Sunday afternoon? That would suit Bruno very well. I could show you a particularly good route that takes nearly three hours to complete.'

'Relief!' Kate exclaimed. 'That doesn't sound scary at all.

But what if it rains?'

'I've thought of that. You can borrow my waterproofs and backpack.'

'What if he hasn't got waterproofs?'

'You can check in advance, and if he hasn't, it's up to him to go shopping.'

'What if he doesn't want to go for a walk?'

Miranda smiled. 'I'm sure Bruno will persuade him.'

This satisfied Kate. 'That's settled then.'

Afterwards their conversation drifted on to other subjects.

Chapter Fifteen

Kate had left the house early, as she had things to see to before visiting her first customer. Miranda's hand hovered over the phone. There was a battle going on inside her. One voice was telling her that speaking to Malcolm would be perfectly straightforward, whereas the other was adamant that she would end up in some kind of inner tangle from which she would not be able to extricate herself.

She paced up and down the room for a few minutes, but this merely served to escalate the intensity of her conflict. She wished Kate was still there, but at the same time she was glad to be alone.

Eventually she took a deep breath, grabbed the phone and keyed in Malcolm's number. It rang several times before inviting her to leave a message.

'Hello, this is Miranda.' Her voice was strong and steady. 'I'm ringing to let you know that I definitely want to go ahead with what we discussed. Can you let me know you've got this message okay?' She finished by giving her number, twice. She would contact her parents once she had heard back from him.

She resumed her research. There was no college today. Her first course was to begin tomorrow afternoon.

Kate returned not long after five o'clock. She burst in through the front door, pretended to stagger as she crossed the room, and then collapsed into a chair.

When she spoke, she sounded euphoric. 'Success! And on more than one front.' She propped her head up and asked, 'How did you get on?'

'If you mean with Malcolm, I phoned and left a message about the room, but I've heard nothing back yet. The rest's been going fine.'

'Nigel and I are going out on Sunday afternoon,' Kate reported triumphantly. 'And Patch is a real sweetie.'

'Patch?'

'My first charge. Here, have a look.' She brought up a picture on her mobile and handed it to Miranda.

Miranda could see that Patch certainly had an endearing look about him. She passed the phone back. 'When did you see him?'

'I had an appointment. Don't you remember?'

'I mean Nigel, not Patch.'

'This morning. I felt so enthused by your plan that I called in to see Nigel after I'd met Patch. Because everything had gone so well, I was feeling really upbeat, and when I suggested the walk, Nigel agreed straight away. I can hardly wait until Sunday, and you must show me that route.'

Miranda took an Ordnance Survey map from her bookcase, and opened it out. Then she showed Kate where to go. 'You can borrow this as well as my waterproofs,' she offered.

'Thanks a lot. I'm parched. I'll put the kettle on. What would you like?'

They were catching up on the lesser news when the phone rang.

'It's bound to be Malcolm,' Kate guessed.

No numbers appeared on the caller display. Instead there was simply the word Withheld. However, Miranda recognised the now familiar voice of Malcolm.

'Hi! Got your message. That's great news. I'll drop a key in to you, and we should make some kind of written agreement so we're both sure where we stand.'

'There's no immediate rush. I can't do anything straight away. Among other things, I'm starting a course in accounting at the college tomorrow afternoon.'

'That means you'll be passing my door. Why not call in on your way back home? I'll be in the office. Things have got into a bit of a muddle, and it'll take me a few hours to sort it out.'

128

Miranda felt a surge of confidence when she replied, 'I'll be with you around half past five.'

When she put the phone down, Kate winked at her. 'That was spot on. It's a pity I've got an evening job on tomorrow. Otherwise, I'd be hanging out of the front door, waiting for you to get back.'

'In that case, I'm very glad you're tied up. I don't want a big fanfare over something that's going to be perfectly straightforward.'

Miranda found the first session on accounting very informative. There were twelve people in the class, all of whom lived locally. Initial introductions revealed a wide spectrum of interests and background. Two were retired people who were expanding their skills in order to be of specific help to voluntary initiatives. Like her, four others had recently been made redundant and were in the process of starting up a small business. The other five had taken early retirement, but were looking for ways of adding to their income. She found the people cheerful and friendly, and felt warmed by the general atmosphere that developed among them. The tutor was excellent. He gave them a thumbnail sketch of his diverse experiences in the business world, and Miranda guessed that he must be at least in his late forties to have achieved so much. His presentation was energetic and enthusiastic. He clearly valued each question from the group, and always sought to give a precise response, often adding background information as well.

She wished that the session was longer, but there was next week to look forward to. Afterwards, one of the older members of the group asked if she needed a lift anywhere.

Miranda smiled. 'That's kind of you, but today I'm meeting a friend not far from here.'

'I'll have the car again next week, so don't hesitate to ask for a run home. In January this time of day is gloomy.'

After the group disbanded, Miranda ambled slowly along the road, her mind full of figures and filing systems. It would take only ten minutes to reach Malcolm's place.

As it came into view, Miranda could see the light from his office window. She looked at her watch. Still more than another ten minutes to go... She slowed her pace, but immediately realised how ridiculous that was, and instead walked straight to the front door.

She knocked a couple of times, opened it, and called, 'Hi! I'm a few minutes early. Will I be disturbing you if I come in?'

There was a clatter that sounded as if something had fallen over, and Malcolm appeared in the hall with a broad grin on his face. 'Come on in. I've been looking forward to seeing you.'

Miranda hesitated for a moment, waiting for the familiar thud of panic to rise inside her, but nothing happened.

'Come on,' Malcolm repeated. 'The place is all warmed up.'

He led the way into his office and offered her the same seat as before. She noticed that the chair behind his desk was lying on its side on the floor. He put it back on its legs and sat down.

'How was the course?' he asked.

Miranda's eyes shone. 'It was excellent. It's a pity I've got to wait a whole week before the next session.'

Malcolm gave her a key ring with two keys on it. 'You'll need both of those to get in,' he explained. 'I've made a few notes here of what we might want in our agreement. Cast your eye over it and see what you think. After we've finalised something, we should get a legal person to look at it.'

'Is that really necessary?'

'It's always best,' Malcolm advised. 'I'm not looking for trouble, but for example, you need to know where you stand if I got run over by a bus.'

Miranda felt slightly embarrassed that she had not thought of this, and she hid her face by leaning over the sheet of paper that Malcolm had handed to her.

'What's the position about insurance?' she asked suddenly. 'You'll be subletting to me. Surely this affects your insurance and your mortgage.'

'I'm looking into it at the moment. I'm certainly not prevented from subletting, but I need to let the providers know the precise circumstances. You'll have to insure your furniture and hangings separately of course.'

'I'll see to that.'

'Why not take that list away with you, and get back to me in a couple of days about any additions or changes to discuss?'

'Yes, I'd prefer that. Malcolm, is there any chance that I could buy a couple of leeks from you before I go?'

'Certainly. Come and choose them from the store.'

He led the way, and pointed to a heap of healthy-looking leeks. 'Take your pick.'

As she stepped forward, her foot caught in something, and she fell. She put out her hands to cushion her fall, but felt herself being lifted back on to her feet.

Malcolm's hands lingered on her waist for a few moments, and she was not certain whether or not he was enjoying that experience, or merely ensuring that she was stable before letting go of her.

'Thanks, I thought I was going to fall flat.'

'It's my pleasure,' he replied, beaming down at her. His smile seemed to carry a special warmth. Miranda was tempted to gaze back at him, but instead selected her leeks. She reached for her purse.

'Have them on the house,' Malcolm told her.

Miranda was about to demur, but changed her mind, and instead replied, 'I'll drop a portion of soup off for you in exchange.'

'I'll enjoy that.' He beamed at her again.

At home, Miranda phoned her parents to let them know the arrangement so far. Her father informed her that he had found a place only ten minutes' drive from her house that had just converted a couple of rooms into a holiday flatlet. Because of the time of year, he had been able to negotiate a favourable deal that extended right up to the Easter holidays. He added that he had enjoyed a lengthy conversation with the owners, who were looking forward to meeting them all.

Afterwards, Miranda skipped around her living space. Her parents would arrive in two weeks' time, and would stay for the whole of February and March.

She spent the rest of the evening making a large quantity of soup, in which the leeks were an essential ingredient. As she worked, she remembered the lovely visit that she had made to Kate's mother's at Christmas.

When Kate came home, rather subdued, Miranda was puzzled.

'What is it?' she asked.

'I had a terrible fright this evening.'

'Sit down and tell me about it.'

'My customer was an ancient German Shepherd. He was a real gentleman, and I love him dearly already.'

'What was the problem?'

'My job was to make friends with him, and to take him for a walk round the block. We'd hardly got past the end of the street, when a huge black mongrel jumped on him and proceeded to sink his fangs straight into my poor Archie.'

'What did you do?'

'I screamed as loudly as I possibly could. Fortunately, a passer-by with a stick came over and beat the black dog off. It eventually ran away with its tail between its legs. I got the name of our rescuer, and then went straight to the out-of-hours vet service. I feel terribly shaken. From now on I'm going to carry a big stick with me. Fortunately Archie's owner was very understanding, but I'm going to get insurance cover tomorrow. I phoned Nigel, and he's going to help me with it.'

'Have you contacted the police?'

'Yes, I did that after I took Archie back home.'

'I'm so glad you weren't hurt,' said Miranda. 'I've made some soup. Would you like some?'

'Is it like Mum's?' Kate asked weakly.

'I've used all the right ingredients... including two leeks

from Malcolm's.'

This information seemed to energise Kate immediately. She sat bolt upright, saying, 'Malcolm! How did you get on?'

Miranda ladled soup into a bowl and handed it to Kate. 'Get that into you, and I'll tell you the news.'

Kate sipped the hot soup.

'I think Malcolm likes me,' Miranda announced.

'I already knew that,' Kate replied, 'but how have you come to that conclusion at last?'

'I can see a number of small signs.'

'That's good. That means you're letting yourself notice what I think has been there for quite a while.'

'And Mum and Dad have found somewhere to stay. They're arriving at the beginning of February.'

'How long will they be here?'

'Two months.'

'I can't wait to meet them.'

'And Dad can't wait to get his hands on the room at Malcolm's.'

'I think that will help to advance things between you and Malcolm.'

'Of course, it will,' Miranda agreed, thinking of her business development.

Kate noticed from Miranda's demeanour that she had skated away from the real point. 'Plague!' she challenged.

Miranda responded angrily. 'What on earth are you going on about?'

Kate stood her ground. 'Miranda, you know very well what I mean.'

Miranda turned away and stirred the soup.

Kate did not intervene.

'I tripped in the vegetable store and he caught me before I fell flat,' Miranda admitted quietly. 'I'm certain he was glad of the opportunity to save me. I must say it felt very nice.'

'A clinch!' Kate teased.

'The trouble is...'

'Go on.'

'The trouble is… now I want it to progress.'

'Great! Tomorrow we can spend a little time working out your next steps.'

'I don't think I need to,' Miranda told her firmly. 'I've got some ideas of my own.'

Chapter Sixteen

It was the end of January. The days were beginning to open out a little, but there was no change in the relentlessly cold weather.

Alongside her efforts to organise resources for her business, Miranda had been studying hard. Not only did she enjoy the subject matter, but also she wanted to be ahead with her reading so that she had more time available to spend with her parents. It was only a few more days before they were due to arrive. The business studies course involved talks by a range of tutors, and was just as exciting for her as the accountancy course.

Kate's services were much in demand, and she was out for hours every day. She noticed that she was becoming very fit, and she liked that. The word had gone round very quickly that she was willing to help out with a range of services as well as pet care. Her smiling face, cheerful attitude and intelligent approach to problems were great assets. Although she made it clear that as yet she had no formal qualifications, this rarely made any difference. She was due to start a ten-week part-time course on care of small animals that would lead to a certificate. But before that she was going on a day's training on how to aid people with reduced mobility. She had decided to go ahead with this because some of her clients were requesting pet care due to their own temporary or long-standing disabilities. Among other things, the icy conditions underfoot had led to a number of broken limbs. Most of her clients were in Branton itself or in its environs, but she didn't rule out going further afield, provided the location could be reached by bus. There were times when neighbours of clients would ask for her help, and she would fit in such requests when she could.

Miranda had become accustomed to calling in on Malcolm on the way home from college. There was hardly ever a time when he wasn't in his office then, and on the rare occasions on which he was called away, he would text her to let her know. They would sit and drink tea. There was always something that they wanted to mull over together. He had cleared the mess out of the back room, had painted it, and was now in the process of moving his bed and clothes into it. He would be in a position to empty the front room by the time Miranda's parents arrived. Miranda had been considering how she would decorate her room, and had shared her ideas with Malcolm, who showed much interest in the project.

Kate had begun to spend a night at Nigel's at the weekends. She would return to Miranda's looking relaxed and content. Miranda asked very little except to enquire about Bruno, an approach that suited Kate well. For her part, she did not try to initiate conversation about Malcolm, although she would tell Miranda to say that she had asked after him. Miranda felt in no hurry to meet Nigel, and likewise Kate had no sense of urgency about meeting Malcolm.

It was during the night before her parents' arrival that Miranda woke from an intense dream. She felt disturbed, and she groped for the light switch. She was glad when the soft glow spread across the room. Kate was at Nigel's, so she was alone.

Three o'clock. She couldn't remember the last time she had been awake at this hour. She switched on the radio for companionship, but the noise it made grated on her, and she silenced it.

She lay there, dozing on and off in the gentle light. Then she found herself fingering her neck with both hands. Why on earth should that be? It was almost as if she were arranging a necklace. Yet she was not wearing one, and had not worn anything like that for some weeks.

She dozed again, but this time she returned to full consciousness with a jolt. Granny Ann's pearls! She got out of bed and fetched them from her jewellery box. Then she fastened them round her neck before getting back into bed.

Somehow she was certain that she had been dreaming about them.

As she warmed up under her duvet, she began to doze again, and this time seemed to slip in and out of a dreamlike state. Sometimes she was small again, sitting on Granny Ann's knee, sometimes she was here, lying in her bed, and sometimes... sometimes, fleetingly, it was as if she were Granny Ann herself. How strange... Who was the secret admirer? She wished she knew. Why hadn't Granny Ann told anyone? After that question came into her mind, she fell into a deep sleep.

When she woke again, the clock showed that it was already after nine. She knew something had happened in the night. Instinctively she touched the pearls round her neck and felt comforted by them. Then she knew in a flash that it had been as if Granny Ann had come to see her, and had come to tell her something.

Surely Granny Ann must have been given these pearls long before she was married. She was the kind of person who would have had no truck with advances from other men once she was engaged. Surely she would have talked about the man who gave her the pearls, *unless it would have been damaging to reveal his identity.* She knew now that she was getting closer to the truth. There had been someone who loved her, but who was not free to be with her. Perhaps it had been the father of one of her charges? How very difficult that would have been. Granny Ann would not have abandoned a child in her care for that, but it would have left her in a very stressful situation. And if that were the case, why had she accepted the pearls?

Whatever their origin, Miranda would always look after these pearls very carefully. 'And if I get married, I shall wear them on my wedding day,' she whispered.

Emily by Mirabelle Maslin

ISBN 978-0-9549551-8-2   £8.99

Orphaned by the age of ten, Emily lives with her Aunt Jane. While preparing to move house, they come across an old diary of Jane's, and she shows Emily some intriguing spiral patterns that appeared in it just before she, Emily, was born. Clearly no passing curiosity, these patterns begin to affect Emily in ways that no one can understand, and as time passes, something momentous begins to form in their lives. While studying at university, Emily meets Barnaby. Sensing that they have been drawn together for a common purpose, they discover that each carries a crucial part of an unfinished puzzle from years past. It is only then that Emily's true purpose is revealed.

Events in 'Emily' are foreshadowed in Mirabelle Maslin's 'Beyond the Veil' and 'Fay'.

Order from your local bookshop, amazon.co.uk or the augurpress website at www.augurpress.com

Beyond the Veil by Mirabelle Maslin
ISBN 0-9549551-4-5   £8.99

Spiral patterns, a strange tape of music from Russia, a 'blank' book and an oddly-carved walking stick...

Ellen encounters Adam, a young widower, and a chain of mysterious and unpredictable events begins to weave their lives together.   Chance, contingency and coincidence all play a part – involving them with friends in profound experiences, and lifting the pall of loss that has been affecting both their lives.

Against a backdrop of music, plant lore, mysterious writing and archaeology, the author touches on deeper issues of bereavement, friendship, illness and the impact of objects from the past on our lives. Altered states, heightened sensitivities and unseen communications are explored, as is the importance of caring and mutual understanding.

The story culminates in an experience of spiritual ecstasy, leading separate paths to an unusual and satisfying convergence.

Order from your local bookshop, amazon, or from the Augur Press website www.augurpress.com

Fay by Mirabelle Maslin
ISBN 0-9549551-3-7   £8.99

Fay is suffering from a mysterious illness.   Her family and friends are
concerned about her.   In her vulnerable state, she begins to be affected by
something more than intuition, and at first no one can make sense of it.

Alongside the preparation for her daughter's wedding, she is drawn into
new situations together with resonances of lives that are long past, and at
last the central meaning of her struggles begins to emerge.

**Order from your local bookshop, amazon, or from the Augur Press
website www.augurpress.com**

The Fifth Key by Mirabelle Maslin

ISBN 978–0–9558936–0–5   £7.99

Soon after Nicholas' thirteenth birthday, his great-uncle John reveals to him a secret – handed down through hundreds of years to the 'chosen one' in every second generation. John is very old. His house has long since fallen into disrepair, and as Nicholas begins to learn about the fifth key and the pledge, John falls ill. Facing these new challenges and helping to repair John's house, Nicholas begins to discover his maturing strengths.

The unexpected appearance of Jake, the traveller whom Nicholas has barely known as his much older brother, heralds a sequence of events that could never have been predicted, and a bond grows between the brothers that evolves beyond the struggles of their ancestors and of Jake's early life.

Order from your local bookshop, amazon.co.uk or the augurpress website at www.augurpress.com

The Candle Flame by Mirabelle Maslin

ISBN 978-0-9558936-1-2   £7.99

One dark winter's night, an unseen force attacks Molly, leaving her for dead. On their return from snaring rabbits, her husband, Sam, and his brothers, James and Alec, discover her, and slowly nurse her back to life. But she cannot speak. Determined to avenge Molly and help her to regain her voice, the brothers search for clues. Could her affliction be due to a curse? The birth of Sam and Molly's son, Nathan, raises questions about his ancestry. Who was Molly's father, and how did he meet his end? Might there be a connection between violent events of long ago and Molly's present state?

Order from your local bookshop, amazon.co.uk or the augurpress website at www.augurpress.com

Also available from Augur Press

The Poetry Catchers	£7.99	978-0-9549551-9-9
by Pupils from Craigton Primary School		
Beyond the Veil by Mirabelle Maslin	£8.99	0-9549551-4-5
Fay by Mirabelle Maslin	£8.99	0-9549551-3-7
Emily by Mirabelle Maslin	£8.99	978-0-9549551-8-2
Hemiplegic Utopia: Manc Style	£6.99	978-0-9549551-7-5
by Lee Seymour		
Carl and other writings by Mirabelle Maslin	£5.99	0-9549551-2-9
Letters to my Paper Lover	£7.99	0-9549551-1-0
by Fleur Soignon		
On a Dog Lead by Mirabelle Maslin	£6.99	978-0-9549551-5-1
Poems of Wartime Years by W N Taylor	£4.99	978-0-9549551-6-8
The Fifth Key by Mirabelle Maslin	£7.99	978-0-9558936-0-5
The Candle Flame by Mirabelle Maslin	£7.99	978-0-9558936-1-2
Mercury in Dental Fillings	£5.99	978-0-9558936-2-9
by Stewart J Wright		
The Voice Within by Catherine Turvey	£5.99	978-0-9558936-3-6
The Supply Teacher's Surprise	£5.99	978-0-9558936-4-3
by Mirabelle Maslin		
For ages 8-14 (and adult readers too):		
Tracy by Mirabelle Maslin	£6.95	0-9549551-0-2

Ordering:	Postage and packing – £1.00 per title
By post	Delf House, 52, Penicuik Road, Roslin, Midlothian EH25 9LH UK
By e-mail	info@augurpress.com
Online	www.augurpress.com (credit cards accepted)

Cheques payable to Augur Press. Prices and availability subject to change without notice. When placing your order, please mention if you do not wish to receive any additional information.

www.augurpress.com

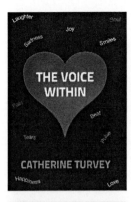

Lightning Source UK Ltd.
Milton Keynes UK
20 November 2010

163146UK00001B/19/P